| DATE | | | |
|---|---|---|---|
| | | | |
| | | | |
| | | | |
| | | | |
| | | | |
| | | | |
| | | | |
| | | | |
| | | | |
| | | | |
| | | | |
| | | | |

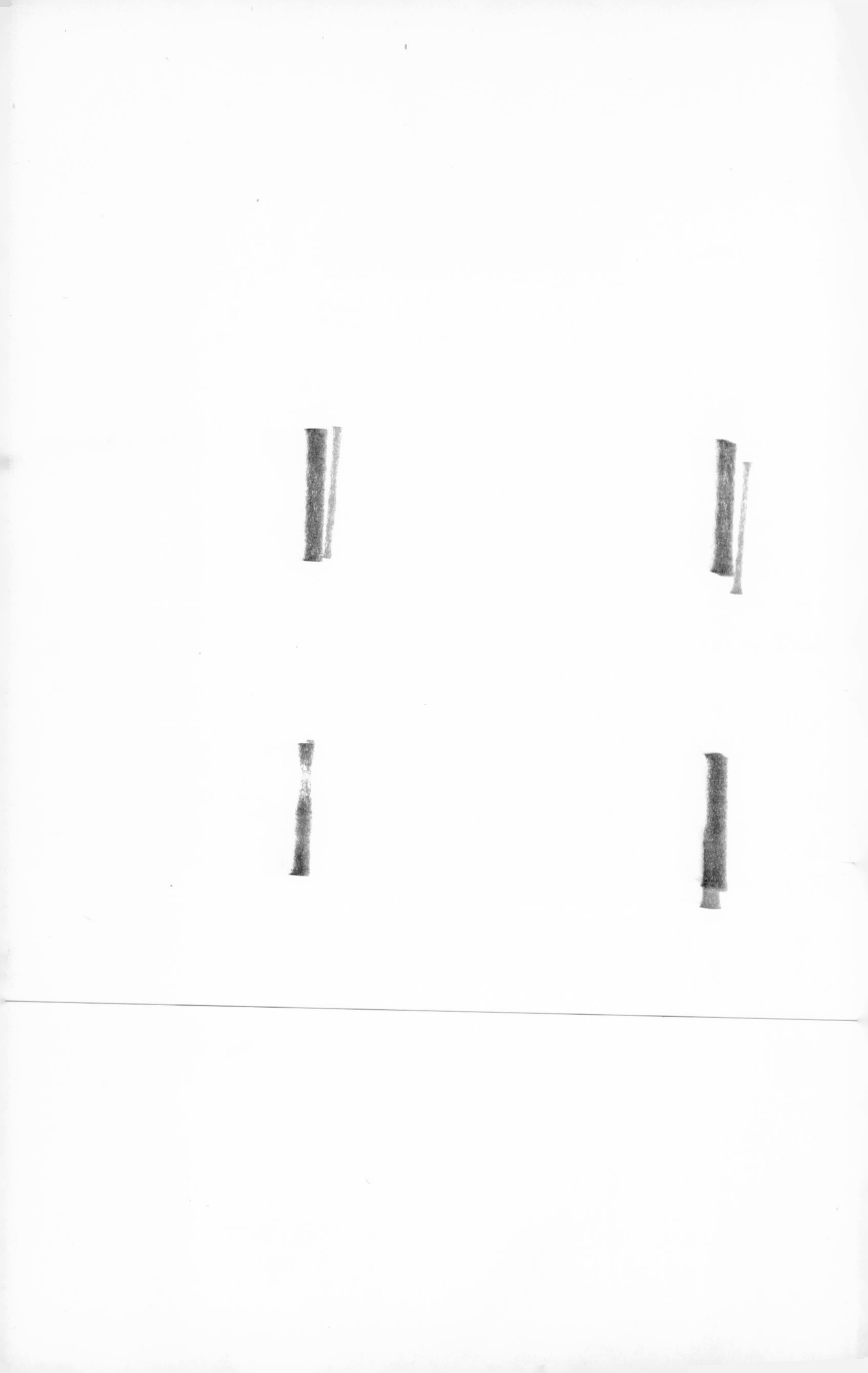

# Horses, Horses, Horses

# Horses, Horses, Horses

A COLLECTION OF STORIES EDITED BY

*Suzanne Wilding*

VAN NOSTRAND REINHOLD COMPANY
NEW YORK CINCINNATI TORONTO LONDON MELBOURNE

*Van Nostrand Reinhold Company Regional Offices:*
*New York Cincinnati Chicago Millbrae Dallas*

*Van Nostrand Reinhold Company International Offices:*
*London Toronto Melbourne*



*Library of Congress Catalog Card Number: 71-110069*
*ISBN 0-442-09451-5*



*Published by Van Nostrand Reinhold Company*
*A Division of Litton Educational Publishing, Inc.*
*450 West 33rd Street, New York, N.Y. 10001*

*Published simultaneously in Canada by*
*Van Nostrand Reinhold Ltd.*

*3 4 5 6 7 8 9 10 11 12 13 14 15 16*

# *Acknowledgments*

"Seeing Eye" reprinted with permission of Charles Scribner's Sons from *Horses I've Known* by Will James. Copyright 1940 Will James; renewal copyright © 1968 Auguste Dufault.

"My Friend Flicka" by Mary O'Hara. Copyright © 1941 by Story Magazine. Reprinted by permission Paul R. Reynolds, Inc., 599 Fifth Ave., New York, N.Y.

"Alcatraz" by Max Brand reprinted by permission of Dodd, Mead & Company, Inc. from *Alcatraz, the Wild Stallion* by Max Brand. Copyright 1923 by Dorothy Faust; copyright renewed 1951 by Dorothy Faust.

"Jim McNab's Story" from *Midnight: Champion Bucking Horse* by Sam Savitt. Copyright © 1957 by Sam Savitt. Reprinted by permission of E. P. Dutton & Co., Inc.

"My Old Man" reprinted with permission of Charles Scribner's Sons from *In Our Time* by Ernest Hemingway. Copyright 1925 Charles Scribner's Sons; renewal copyright 1953 by Ernest Hemingway.

Excerpts from "Look of Eagles," from *Hoofbeats* by John Taintor Foote by permission of Appleton-Century, affiliate of Meredith Press. Copyright 1916 by D. Appleton & Co. Copyright 1950 by John Taintor Foote.

"The Race" from *The Will to Win* by Jane McIlvaine. Copyright © 1966 by Jane McIlvaine McClary. Reprinted by permission of Doubleday & Company, Inc.

"Introduction to Modern American Fox Hunting" by special arrangement with original publisher. Copyright © 1953 Time Inc.

"How the Brigadier Slew the Fox" from *Adventures of Gerard* by Sir Arthur Conan Doyle. Reprinted by permission of the Estate of Sir Arthur Conan Doyle.

"Peter" by Gordon Grand from *The Millbeck Hounds.* Reprinted by permission of the executor of the author's estate.

"The Tale of Anthony Bell" by Sir Alfred Munnings K.C.V.O. President of the Royal Academy London 1944-1949. From *Ballads and Poems.*

"Florian Performs for Franz Joseph" from *Florian* by Felix Salten. By permission of Albert Muller Verlag. All rights reserved.

"The Farm Horse That Became a Champion" by Philip B. Kunhardt. Reprinted with permission from the July 1960 Reader's Digest. Copyright 1960 by The Reader's Digest Assn., Inc. Condensed from Farmer's Advocate.

"The Will" from *A Kingdom in a Horse* by Maia Wojciechowska. Copyright © 1965 by Maia Wojciechowska Rodman. Reprinted with permission of Harper & Row, Publishers.

*To A.M.D.B.*
*Whose taste in sporting literature and sporting art has been my greatest influence, this book is lovingly dedicated.*

# *Contents*

# *Introduction*

*Everything pleasant that has ever happened to me has had something to do with a horse. So it was not surprising that, when I started to write children's books, I wrote about horses. The subject of my first anthology is about the same noble animal.*

*I did not come from a horsy family and I had to work hard for my early riding one short hour a week at a stable in Westchester County, New York. Since then, I have been fortunate enough to own my own horse and, in the last few years, to hack and hunt in Chester County, Pennsylvania, over some of the most beautiful country in the U.S. But it isn't necessary to ride a horse to enjoy reading about them.*

*What I have tried to do in this volume is to touch the high spots of good writing, laced with sound equine information about Western riding, racing, fox hunting, and a few non-categorized stories which I have gathered together under the title of Fact & Fiction.*

*Due to limitations of space, I have only been able to include a taste of each, but if "The Seeing Eye" makes you realize that the first prerequisite of writing is a thorough knowledge of your subject; if "My Old Man" turns you into a student of Heming-*

*way; if "How the Brigadier Slew the Fox" encourages you to read the whole of the Brigadier Gerard series; if "Snow Man" persuades you to attend your first horse show—my purpose has been fulfilled.*

*I hope that this book will give you many hours of pleasure, but I also hope it will intrigue you enough to make you want to learn more about equine literature and every phase in the life of one of man's best friends, the horse.*

# WESTERN

# The Seeing Eye

## *by Will James*

*Will James, one of our best loved writers of cowboy stories, had no formal schooling. He was born in a covered wagon in Montana in 1892 and spent most of his life on the open range.*

*As a small boy, he began to draw on a writing tablet if he had one, and with a stick in the dirt if no paper was available. James drew long before he could read and write, but after he had mastered the ABCs, he tried setting pictures down in words; not because he thought he had any great writing talent, but because he hoped they would help sell his drawings of the West.*

*His career was varied. He never liked staying in one place for long and earned his living rough riding, being a cowhand, a trapper, and a sometime cattle rustler. On two occasions he tangled with the mounties and spent several miserable months in a Canadian jail. After he was cleared of guilt in a barroom brawl, he never tampered with the law again.*

*By the time he was thirty, broncbusting had all but crippled James. He married the sister of one of his cowboy buddies and longed to settle down and earn his living as an aritst.*

*He sold a few pictures, but his real success came when he wrote stories of the West and illustrated them. He wrote the way a cow-*

*boy talks, and although the lack of grammar is not always desirable, the man, who never saw the inside of a school room, won the Newberry medal for* Smoky the Cow Horse, *the most coveted award for American literature for children.*

*He died in 1942.*

It's worse than tough for anybody to be blind, but I don't think it's as tough for an indoor born and raised person, as it is for one whose life is with the all out-of-doors the most of his life from childhood on. The outdoor man misses his freedom to roam over the hills and the sight of 'em ever changing. A canary would die outside his cage, but a free-born eagle would dwindle away inside of one.

Dane Gruger was very much of an out-of-door man. He was born on a little ranch along a creek bottom, in the heart of the cow country, growed up with it to be a good cowboy; then, like with his dad, went on in the cow business. A railroad went through the lower part of the ranch, but stations and little towns was over twenty miles away either way.

He had a nice little spread when I went to work for him, was married and had two boys who done some of the riding. I'd been riding for Dane for quite a few days before I knew he was blind; not totally blind but, as his boys told me, he couldn't see any further than his outstretched hand, and that was blurred. He couldn't read, not even big print, with any kind of glasses, so he never wore any.

That's what fooled me, and he could look you "right square in the eye" while talking to you. What was more he'd go straight down to the corral, catch his horse, saddle him and ride away like any man with full sight. The thing I first noticed and wondered at was that he never rode with us, and after the boys told me, I could understand. It was that he'd be of no use out on the range and away from the ranch.

Dane had been blind a few years when I come there and he'd of course got to know every foot of the ten miles which the ranch covered on the creek bottom before that happened. The ranch itself was one to two miles wide in some places and taking in some brakes. The whole of that was fenced and cross-fenced into pastures and hay lands, and Dane knew to within an inch when he came to every fence, gate or creek crossing. He knew how many head of cattle or horses might be in each pasture, how all was faring, when some broke out or some broke in, and where. He could find bogged cattle, a cow with young calf needing help, and know everything that went well or wrong with what stock would be held on the ranch.

He of course seldom could do much toward helping whatever stock needed it or fixing the holes he found in the fences, but when he'd get back to the ranch house he could easy tell the boys when there was anything wrong and the exact spot where, in which field or pasture, how far from which side of the creek of what fence, and what all the trouble might be. It would then be up to the boys to set things to rights, and after Dane's description of the spot it was easy found.

During the time I was with that little outfit I got to know Dane pretty well, well enough to see that I don't think he could of lived if he hadn't been able to do what he was doing. He was so full of life and gumption and so appreciating of all around him that he could feel, hear and breathe in. I'd sometimes see him hold his horse to a standstill while he only listened to birds or the faraway bellering of cattle, even to the yapping of prairie dogs, which most cowboys would rather not hear the sound of.

To take him away from all of that, the open air, the feel of his saddle and horse under him, and set him on a chair to do nothing but sit and babble and think, would of brought a quick end to him.

With the riding he done he felt satisfied he was doing something worth doing instead of just plain riding. He wouldn't of cared for that, and fact was, he well took the place of an average rider.

But he had mighty good help in the work he was doing, and that was the two horses he used, for they was both as well trained to his wants and care as the dogs that's used nowadays to lead the blind and which are called "The Seeing Eye."

Dane had the advantage over the man with the dog, for he didn't have to walk and use a cane at every step. He rode, and he had more confidence in his horses' every step than he had in his own, even if he could of seen well. As horses do, they naturally sensed every foot of the earth under 'em without ever looking down at it, during sunlight, darkness or under drifted snow.

Riding into clumps of willows or thickets which the creek bottoms had much of, either of the two horses was careful to pick out a wide enough trail through so their rider wouldn't get scratched or brushed off. If they come to a place where the brush was too thick and Dane was wanting to go through that certain thicket, the ponies, regardless of his wants, would turn back for a ways and look for a better opening. Dane never argued with 'em at such times. He would just sort of head 'em where he wanted to go and they'd do the rest to pick out the best way there.

Them horses was still young when I got to that outfit, seven and eight years of age, and would be fit for at least twenty years more with the little riding and good care they was getting. Dane's boys had broke 'em especially for their dad's use that way and they'd done a fine job of it.

One of the horses, a gray of about a thousand pounds, was called Little Eagle. That little horse never missed a thing in sight or sound. With his training, the rustling of the brush close by would make him investigate and learn the cause before leaving that spot. Dane would know by his actions whether it was a newborn calf that had been hid or some cow in distress. It was the same at the boggy places along the creek or alkali swamps. If Little Eagle rode right on around and without stopping, Dane knew that all was well. If he stopped at any certain spot, bowed his neck and snorted low, then Dane knew that some horse or cow was in trouble. Keeping his hand on Little Eagle's neck he'd have him go on; and by the bend of that horse's neck as he went, like pointing, Dane could tell the exact location of where that animal was that was in trouble, or whatever it was that was wrong.

Sometimes, Little Eagle would line out on a trot of his own accord, and as though there was something needed looking into right away. At times he'd even break into a lope, and then Dane wouldn't know what to expect, whether it was stock breaking through a fence, milling around an animal that was down, or what. But most always it would be when a bunch of stock, horses or cattle, would be stringing out in single file, maybe going to water or some other part of the pasture.

At such times Little Eagle would get just close enough to the stock so Dane could count 'em by the sounds of the hoofs going by, a near-impossible thing to do for a man that can see, but Dane got so he could do it and get a mighty close count on what stock was in each pasture that way. Close enough so he could tell if any had got out or others got in.

With the horses in the pastures, there was bells on the leaders of every bunch and some on one of every little bunch that sort of held together and separate from others. Dane knew by the sound of every bell which bunch it was and about how many there would be to each. The boys kept him posted on that, every time they'd run a bunch in for some reason or other. Not many horses was ever kept under fence, but there was quite a few of the purebred cattle for the upbreeding of the outside herds.

At this work of keeping tab on stock, Little Eagle was a cowboy by himself. With his natural intellect so developed as to what was wanted of him, he could near tell of what stock was wanted or not and where they belonged. The proof of that was when he turned a bunch of cattle out of a hayfield one time, and other times, and drove 'em to the gate of the field where they'd broke out of, circled around 'em when the gate was reached and went to it for Dane to open. He then drove the cattle through; none got away, not from Little Eagle, and Dane would always prepare to ride at such times, for if any did try to break away Little Eagle would be right on their tail to bring 'em back, and for a blind man, not knowing when his horse is going to break into a sudden run, stop or turn, that's kind of hard riding, on a good cow horse.

About all Dane would have to go by most of the time was the feel of the top muscles on Little Eagle's neck, and he got to know by them about the same as like language to him. With one hand most always on them muscles, he felt what the horse seen. Tenseness, wonder, danger, fear, relaxation and about all that a human feels at the sight of different things. Places, dangerous or smooth, trouble or peace.

Them top muscles told him more, and more plainly than if another rider had been riding constantly alongside of him and telling him right along of what he seen. That was another reason why Dane liked to ride alone. He felt more at ease, no confusion, and wasn't putting anybody out of their way by talking and describing when they maybe wouldn't feel like it.

And them two horses of Dane's, they not only took him wherever he wanted to go but never overlooked any work that needed to be done. They took it onto themselves to look for work which, being they always felt so good, was like play to them. Dane knew it when such times comes and he then would let 'em go as they chose.

Neither of the horses would of course go out by themselves without a rider and do that work. They wouldn't of been interested in doing that without Dane's company. What's more they couldn't have opened the gates that had to be gone through and besides they wasn't wanted to do that. They was to be the company of Dane and with him in whatever he wanted to do.

Dane's other horse was a trim bay about the same size as Little

Eagle, and even though just as good, he had different ways about him. He was called Ferret, and a ferret he was for digging up and finding out things, like a cow with new-born calf or mare with colt, and he was even better than Little Eagle for finding holes in fences or where some was down.

All that came under the special training the boys had given him and Little Eagle, and if it wasn't for automobiles these days, such as them would be mighty valuable companions in the city, even more useful in the streets than the dog is; for the horse would soon know where his rider would want to go after being ridden such places a few times.

Unlike most horses it wasn't these two's nature to keep wanting to turn back to the ranch (home) when Dane would ride 'em away, and they wouldn't turn back until they knew the ride was over and it was time to. Sometimes Dane wouldn't show up for the noon meal, and that was all right with the ponies too, for he'd often get off of 'em and let 'em graze with reins dragging. There was no danger of either of them ever leaving Dane, for they seemed as attached to him as any dog could be to his master.

It was the same way with Dane for them, and he had more confidence in their trueness and senses than most humans have in one another.

A mighty good test and surprising outcome of that came one day as a powerful big cloudburst hit above the ranch a ways and left Dane acrost the creek from home. The creek had turned into churning wild waters the size of a big river in a few minutes, half a mile wide in some places and licking up close to the higher land where the ranch buildings and corrals was.

It kept on a-raining hard after the cloudburst had fell and it didn't act like it was going to let up for some time, and the wide river wouldn't be down to creek size or safe to cross, at least not for a day or so.

The noise of the rushing water was a-plenty to let Dane know of the cloudburst. It had come with a sudden roar and without a drop of warning, and Dane's horse, he was riding Little Eagle that day, plainly let him know the danger of the wide stretch of swirling fast waters. It wasn't the danger of the water only, but uprooted trees and all kinds of heavy timber speeding along would make the crossing more than dangerous, not only dangerous but it would about mean certain death.

Little Eagle would of tackled the swollen waters or anything Dane would of wanted him to, but Dane knew a whole lot better than to make that wise horse go where he didn't want to, any time.

Dane could tell by the noise, and riding to the edge of the water and the location where he was, how wide the body of wild waters was. He knew that the stock could keep out of reach of it on either side without being jammed against the fences, but he got worried about the ranch, wondering if the waters had got up to the buildings. He worried too about his family worrying about him, and maybe trying to find and get to him.

That worrying got him to figuring on ways of getting back. He sure couldn't stay where he was until the waters went down, not if he could help it. It wouldn't be comfortable being out so long in the heavy rain either, even if he did have his slicker on, and it wouldn't do to try to go to the neighbor's ranch which was some fifteen miles away. He doubted if he could find it anyway, for it was acrost a bunch of rolling hills, nothing to go by, and Little Eagle wouldn't know that *there* would be where Dane would be wanting him to go. Besides there was the thought of his family worrying so about him and maybe risking their lives in trying to find him.

He'd just have to get home somehow, and it was at the thought of his neighbor's ranch, and picturing the distance and country to it in his mind, that he thought of the railroad, for he would of had to cross it to get there. And then, thinking of the railroad, the thought came of the trestle crossing along it and over the creek. Maybe he could make that. That would be sort of a dangerous crossing too, but the more he thought of it the more he figured it worth taking the chances of trying. That was the only way of his getting on the other side of the high waters and back to the ranch.

The railroad and trestle was only about half a mile from where he now was, and that made it all the more tempting to try. So after thinking it over in every way, including the fact that he'd be taking chances with losing his horse also, he finally decided to take the chance, at the risk of both himself and his horse—that is, if his horse seen it might be safe enough. He felt it had to be done and it could be done, and there went to show his faith and confidence in that Little Eagle horse of his.

And that confidence sure wasn't misplaced, for a coolerheaded, brainier horse never was.

There was two fences to cross to get to the railroad and trestle, and it wasn't at all necessary to go through gates to get there, for the swollen water with jamming timbers had laid the fence down for quite a ways on both sides of the wide river, some of the wire strands to break and snap and coil all directions.

A strand of barbed wire, even if flat to the ground, is a mighty dangerous thing to ride over, for a horse might pick it up with a hoof, and as most horses will scare, draw their hind legs up under 'em and act up. The result might be a wicked sawing wire cut at the joint by the hock, cutting veins and tendons and often crippling a horse for life. In such cases the rider is also very apt to get tangled up in the wire, for that wicked stuff seems to have the ways of the tentacles of a devilfish at such times.

Loose wire laying around on the ground is the cowboy's worst fear, especially so with Dane, for, as he couldn't see, it was many times more threatening as he rode most every day from one fenced-in field to the other. But the confidence he had in his two coolheaded ponies relieved him of most all his fear of the dangerous barbed wire, and either one of 'em would stop and snort a little at the sight of a broken strand coiled to the ground. Dane knew what that meant and it always brought a chill to his spine. He'd get down off his saddle, feel around carefully in front of his horse, and usually the threatening coil would be found to within a foot or so of his horse's nose. The coil would then be pulled and fastened to the fence, to stay until a ranch hand, with team and buckboard, would make the rounds of all fences every few months and done a general fixing of 'em.

It's too bad barbed wire *has* to be used for fences. It has butchered and killed many good horses, and some riders. But barbed wire is about the only kind of fence that will hold cattle most of the time, and when there has to be many long miles of it, even with the smaller ranches, that's about the only kind of fence that can be afforded or used. Cattle (even the wildest) seldom get a scratch by it, even in breaking through a four-strand fence of it or going over it while it's loose and coiled on the ground, for they don't get rattled when in wire as a horse does, and they hold their hind legs straight back when going through, while the horse draws 'em under him instead and goes to tearing around.

Both Little Eagle and Ferret had been well trained against scaring and fighting wire if they ever got into it, also trained not to get into it, and stop whenever coming to some that was loose on the ground. That training had been done with a rope and a piece of smooth wire at one end, and being they was naturally coolheaded they soon learned all the tricks of the wire and how to behave when they come near any of that coiled on the ground.

There was many such coils as the flood waters rampaged along the creek bottom, and as Dane headed Little Eagle toward the railroad and trestle he then let him pick his own way through and around the two fence entanglements on the way there, along the edge of the rushing water.

Little Eagle done considerable winding around and careful stepping as he come to the fences that had been snapped and washed to scattering, dangerous strands over the field. Dane gave him his time, let him go as he chose, and finally the roar of the waters against the high banks by the trestle came to his ears. It sounded as though it was near up to the trestle, which he knew was plenty high, and that gave him a good idea of what a cloud-burst it had been.

He then got mighty dubious about trying to cross the trestle, for it was a long one, there was no railing of any kind on the sides, and part of it might be under water or even washed away. There was some of the flood water in the ditch alongside the railroad grade and it wasn't so many feet up it to the track level.

Riding between the rails a short ways he come to where the trestle begun and there he stopped Little Eagle. The swirling waters made a mighty roar right there, and how he wished he could of been able to see then, more than any time since his blindness had overtook him.

Getting off Little Eagle there, he felt his way along to the first ties to the trestle and the space between each, which was about five inches and just right for Little Eagle's small hoofs to slip in between, Dane thought. One such a slip would mean a broken leg, and the horse have to be shot right there, to lay between the rails. The rider would be mighty likely to go over the side of the trestle, too.

Dane hardly had any fear for himself, but he did have for Little Eagle. Not that he feared he would put a foot between the ties, for that little horse was too wise, coolheaded and careful to do anything like that, Dane knew. What worried him most was if the trestle was still up and above water all the way acrost. There would be no turning back, for in turning is when Little Eagle would be mighty liable to slip a hoof between the ties. The rain had let up but the wind was blowing hard and the tarred ties was slippery as soaped glass.

It all struck Dane as fool recklessness to try to cross that long and narrow trestle at such a time, but he felt he should try, and to settle his dubiousness he now left it to Little Eagle and his good sense as to whether to tackle it or not.

If he went he would *ride* him across, not try to crawl, feel his way and lead him, for in leading the horse he wouldn't be apt to pay as much attention to his footing and to nosing every dangerous step he made. Besides, Dane kind of felt that if Little Eagle should go over the side he'd go with him.

So, getting into the saddle again, he let Little Eagle stand for a spell, at the same time letting him know that he wanted to cross the trestle, for him to size it up and see if it could be done. It was up to him, and the little gray well understood.

It might sound unbelievable, but a good sensible horse and rider have a sort of feel-language which is mighty plain between 'em, and when comes a particular dangerous spot the two can discuss the possibilities of getting over or acrost it as well as two humans can, and even better, for the horse has the instinct which the human lacks. He can tell danger where the human can't, and the same with the safety.

It was that way with Little Eagle and Dane, only even more so, because as Little Eagle, like Ferret, had been trained to realize Dane's affliction, cater and sort of take care of him, they was always watchful. Then with Dane's affection and care for them, talking to 'em and treating 'em like the true pardners they was, there was an understanding and trust between man and horse that's seldom seen between man and man.

Sitting in his saddle with his hand on Little Eagle's neck the two "discussed" the dangerous situation ahead in such a way that the loud roar of the water foaming by and under the trestle didn't interfere any with the decision that was to come.

There was a tenseness in the top muscles of Little Eagle's neck as he looked over the scary, narrow, steel-ribboned trail ahead, nervous at the so-careful investigation, that all sure didn't look well. But Dane'd now left it all to Little Eagle's judgment, and just as he had about expected he'd be against trying, Little Eagle, still all tense and quivering some, planted one foot on the first tie, and crouching a bit, all nerves and muscles steady, started on the way of the dangerous crossing.

Every step by step from the first seemed like a long minute to Dane. The brave little horse, his nose close to the ties, at the same time looking ahead, was mighty careful how he placed each front foot, and sure that the hind one would come up to the exact same place afterward, right where that front one had been. He didn't just plank his hoof and go on, but felt for a sure footing on the wet and slippery tarred ties before putting any weight on it and making another step. Something like a mountain climber, feeling and making sure of his every hold while going on with his climbing.

The start wasn't the worst of the crossing. That begin to come as they went further along and nearer to the center. There, with the strong wind blowing broadside of 'em, the swift waters churning, sounding like to the level of the slippery ties, would seem about scary enough to chill the marrow in any being. But there was more piled onto that, for as they neared the center it begin to tremble and sway as if by earth tremors. This was by the high rushing waters swirling around the tall and now submerged supporting timbers.

Little Eagle's step wasn't so sure then, and as careful as he was, there come a few times when he slipped, and a time or two when a hoof went down between the ties, leaving him to stand on three shaking legs until he got his hoof up and on footing again.

With most any other horse it would of been the end of him and his rider right then. As it was, Little Eagle went on, like a tightrope walker, with every muscle at work. And Dane, riding mighty light on him, his heart up his throat at every slip or loss of footing, done his best not to get him off balance but help him that way when he thought he could.

If the shaking, trembling and swaying of the trestle had been steady it would of been less scary and some easier, but along with the strong vibrations of the trestle there'd sometimes come a big uprooted tree to smash into it at a forty-mile speed. There'd be a quiver all along the trestle at the impact. It would sway and bend dangerously, to slip back again as the tree would be washed under and on.

Such goings-on would jar Little Eagle's footing to where he'd again slip a hoof between the ties, and Dane would pray, sometimes cuss a little. But the way Little Eagle handled his feet and every part of himself, sometimes on the tip of his toes, the sides of his hoofs and even to his knees, he somehow managed to keep right side up.

Good thing, Dane thought, that the horse wasn't shod, for shoes without sharp calks would have been much worse on than none, on the slippery ties. As it was, and being his shoes had been pulled off only a couple of days before to ease his feet some between shoeings, his hoofs was sharp at the edges and toe, and that gave him more chance.

The scary and most dangerous part of the trestle was reached, the center, and it was a good thing maybe that Dane couldn't see while Little Eagle sort of juggled himself over that part, for the trestle had been under repair and some of the old ties had been taken away in a few places, to later be replaced by new ones; but where each tie had been taken away, that left an opening of near two feet wide. Mighty scary for Little Eagle too, but he eased over them gaps without Dane knowing.

Dane felt as though it was long weary miles and took about that much time to finally get past the center and most dangerous part of the five-hundred-yard trestle, for them five hundred yards put more wear on him during that time than five hundred miles would of.

And he was far from near safe going as yet, for he'd just passed center and the trestle was still doing some tall trembling and dangerous weaving, when, as bad and spooky as things already was, there come the sound of still worse fear and danger, and Dane's heart stood still. It was a train whistle he'd heard above the roar of the waters. It sounded like the train was coming his way, facing him, and there'd sure be no chance for him to turn and make it back, for he'd crossed over half of the trestle, the worst part, and going back would take a long time.

All the dangers and fears piling together now, instead of exciting Dane, seemed to cool and steady him, like having to face the worst and make the best of it. He rode right on toward the coming train.

He knew from memory that the railroad run a straight line to the trestle, that there was no railroad crossing nor other reason for the engineer to blow his whistle, unless it was for him, himself. Then it came to him that the engineer must of seen him on the trestle and would sure stop his train, if he could.

Standing up in his stirrups he raised his big black hat high as he could and waved it from side to side as a signal for the engineer to stop his train. Surely they could see that black hat of his and realize the predicament he was in. That getting off the trestle would mean almost certain death.

But the train sounded like it was coming right on, and at that Dane wondered if maybe it was coming too fast to be able to stop. He got a little panicky then, and for a second he was about to turn Little Eagle off the trestle and swim for it. It would of been a long and risky swim, maybe carried for miles down country before they could of reached either bank, and it would of taken more than luck to've succeeded. But if they'd got bowled over by some tree trunk and went down the churning waters that would be better, Dane thought, than to have Little Eagle smashed to smithereens by by the locomtive. He had no thought for himself.

About the only thing that made him take a bigger chance and

ride on some more was that he knew that the whole train and its crew would be doomed before it got halfways on the trestle, and what if it was a passenger train?

At that thought he had no more fear of Little Eagle keeping his footing on the trestle. His fear now went for the many lives there might be on the train, and he sort of went wild and to waving his big black hat all the more in trying to warn of the danger.

But he didn't put on no such action as to unbalance the little gray in any way. He still felt and helped with his every careful step, and then there got to be a prayer with each one, like with the beads of the rosary.

He rubbed his moist eyes and also prayed he could see, now of all times and if only just for this once, and then the train whistle blew again, so close this time that it sounded like it was on the trestle, like coming on, and being mighty near to him.—Dane had done his best, and now was his last and only chance to save Little Eagle and himself, by sliding off the trestle. He wiped his eyes like as though to see better, and went to reining Little Eagle off the side of the trestle. But to his surprise, Little Eagle wouldn't respond to the rein. It was the first time excepting amongst the thick brush or bad creek crossings that horse had ever went against his wishes that way. But this was now very different, and puzzled, he tried him again and again, with no effect, and then, all at once, *he could see.*

Myself and one of Dane's boys had been riding, looking for Dane soon after the cloudburst hit, and seeing the stopped passenger train with the many people gathered by the engine, we high-loped toward it, there to get the surprise of seeing Dane on Little Eagle on the trestle and carefully making each and every dangerous step toward us and solid ground.

We seen we sure couldn't be of no use to the little gray nor Dane, only maybe a hindrance, and being there was only a little ways more we held our horses and watched. Looking on the length of the trestle we noticed that only the rails and ties showed above the high water; there was quite a bend in it from the swift and powerful pressure, and the rails and ties was leaning, like threatening to break loose at any time.

How the little horse and Dane ever made it, with the strong wind, slippery ties and all a-weaving, was beyond us. So was it with the passengers who stood with gaping mouths and tense watching. What if they'd known that the rider had been blind while he made the dangerous crossing?

And as the engineer went on to tell the spellbound passengers how that man and horse on the trestle had saved all their lives, they was more than thankful, for as the heavy cloudburst had come so sudden and hit in one spot, there'd been no report of it, and as the engineer said, he might of drove onto the trestle a ways before knowing. Then it would of been too late.

But Little Eagle was the one who played the biggest part in stopping what would have been a terrible happening. He was the one who decided to make the dangerous crossing, the one who had to use his head and hoofs with all his skill and power, also the one who at the last of the stretch would not heed Dane's pull of the reins to slide off the trestle. His first time not to do as he was wanted to. He'd disobeyed and had saved another life. He'd been "The Seeing Eye."

The fuss over with as Dane finally rode up on solid ground and near the engine, we then was the ones due for a big surprise. For Dane *spotted* us out from the crowd, and smiling, rode straight for us and looked us both square in the eye.

The shock and years he lived crossing that trestle, then the puzzling over Little Eagle not wanting to turn at the touch of the rein had done the trick, had brought his sight back.

After that day, Little Eagle and Ferret was sort of neglected, neglected knee-deep in clover, amongst good shade and where clear spring water run. The seeing eyes was partly closed in contentment.

# My Friend Flicka

*from* THE ORIGINAL SHORT STORY

*by Mary O'Hara*

*No American horse anthology is complete without a story from one of Mary O'Hara's novels, and I am proud to include the original short story of* My Friend Flicka *in these pages.*

My Friend Flicka, *perhaps her greatest novel, began quietly enough in* Story *Magazine. It didn't stay there long and entered the hardcover ranks by being included in the O. Henry Memorial Award Prize Stories of 1941. It had such appeal that the author was persuaded to develop it into a full-length bestseller and later into a movie.*

*Mary O'Hara, though she was born in Brooklyn, gained fame through her stories of the West. Her father was an Episcopal minister; her ancestry traces back to William Penn and Jonathan Edwards. She went to New England schools and then to Europe, where she studied languages and music. Her musical compositions were published long before she became a noted writer.*

*Upon her return from Europe, she moved to California and wrote for the movies, but after her marriage she and her husband settled on a ranch in Wyoming. Here is where she developed her love of horses and started to write* My Friend Flicka, *which today is considered an adult as well as a young people's classic.*

Report cards for the second semester were sent out soon after school closed in mid-June.

Kennie's was a shock to the whole family.

"If I could have a colt all for my own," said Kennie, "I might do better."

Rob McLaughlin glared at his son. "Just as a matter of curiosity," he said, "how do you go about it to get a *zero* in an examination? Forty in arithmetic; seventeen in history! But a *zero?* Just as one man to another, what goes on in your head?"

"Yes, tell us how you do it, Ken," chirped Howard.

"Eat your breakfast, Howard," snapped his mother.

Kennie's blond head bent over his plate until his face was almost hidden. His cheeks burned.

McLaughlin finished his coffee and pushed his chair back. "You'll do an hour a day on your lessons all through the summer."

Nell McLaughlin saw Kennie wince as if something had actually hurt him.

Lessons and study in the summertime, when the long winter was just over and there weren't hours enough in the day for all the things he wanted to do!

Kennie took things hard. His eyes turned to the wide-open window with a look almost of despair.

The hill opposite the house, covered with arrow-straight jack pines, was sharply etched in the thin air of the eight-thousand-foot altitude. Where it fell away, vivid green grass ran up to meet it; and over range and upland poured the strong Wyoming sunlight that stung everything into burning color. A big jack rabbit sat under one of the pines, waving his long ears back and forth.

Ken had to look at his plate and blink back tears before he could turn to his father and say carelessly, "Can I help you in the corral with the horses this morning, Dad?"

"You'll do your study every morning before you do anything

else." And McLaughlin's scarred boots and heavy spurs clattered across the kitchen floor. "I'm disgusted with you. Come. Howard."

Howard strode after his father, nobly refraining from looking at Kennie.

"Help me with the dishes, Kennie," said Nell McLaughlin as she rose, tied on a big apron, and began to clear the table.

Kennie looked at her in despair. She poured steaming water into the dishpan and sent him for the soap powder.

"If I could have a colt," he muttered again.

"Now get busy with that dish towel, Ken. It's eight o'clock. You can study till nine and then go up to the corral. They'll still be there.

At supper that night Kennie said, "But Dad, Howard had a colt all of his own when he was only eight. And he trained it and schooled it all himself; and now he's eleven, and Highboy is three, and he's riding him. I'm nine now and even if you did give me a colt now I couldn't catch up to Howard because I couldn't ride it till it was a three-year-old and then I'd be twelve."

Nell laughed. "Nothing wrong with that arithmetic."

But Rob said, "Howard never gets less than seventy-five average at school, and hasn't disgraced himself and his family by getting more demerits than any other boy in his class."

Kennie didn't answer. He couldn't figure it out. He tried hard; he spent hours poring over his books. That was supposed to get you good marks, but it never did. Everyone said he was bright. Why was it that when he studied he didn't learn? He had a vague feeling that perhaps he looked out the window too much, or looked through the walls to see clouds and sky and hills and wonder what was happening out there. Sometimes it wasn't even a wonder, just a pleasant drifting feeling of nothing at all, as if nothing mattered, as if there was always plenty of time, as if the lessons would get done of themselves. And then the bell would ring, and study period was over.

If he had a colt . . .

When the boys had gone to bed that night Nell McLaughlin sat down with her overflowing mending basket and glanced at her husband.

He was at his desk as usual, working on account books and inventories.

Nell threaded a darning needle and thought, "It's either that whacking big bill from the vet for the mare that died or the last half of the tax bill."

It didn't seem just the auspicious moment to plead Kennie's cause. But then, these days, there was always a line between Rob's eyes and a harsh note in his voice.

"Rob," she began.

He flung down his pencil and turned around.

"Damn that law!" he exclaimed.

"What law?"

"The state law that puts high taxes on pedigreed stock. I'll have to do as the rest of 'em do—drop the papers."

"Drop the papers! But you'll never get decent prices if you don't have registered horses."

"I don't get decent prices now."

"But you will someday if you don't drop the papers."

"Maybe." He bent again over the desk.

Rob, thought Nell, was a lot like Kennie himself. He set his heart. Oh, how stubbornly he set his heart on just some one thing he wanted above everything else. He had set his heart on horses and ranching way back when he had been a crack rider at West Point; and he had resigned and thrown away his army career just for the horses. Well, he'd got what he wanted. . . .

She drew a deep breath, snipped her thread, laid down the sock, and again looked across at her husband as she unrolled another length of darning cotton.

To get what you want is one thing, she was thinking. The three-thousand-acre ranch and the hundred head of horses. But to make it pay—for a dozen or more years they had been trying to make it pay. People said ranching hadn't paid since the beef barons ran their herds on public land; people said the only prosperous ranchers in Wyoming were the dude ranchers; people said . . .

But suddenly she gave her head a little rebellious, gallant shake. Rob would always be fighting and struggling against something, like Kennie; perhaps like herself, too. Even those first years when there was no water piped into the house, when every day brought a new difficulty or danger, how she had loved it! How she still loved it!

She ran the darning ball into the toe of a sock, Kennie's sock. The length of it gave her a shock. Yes, the boys were growing up fast, and now Kennie—Kennie and the colt . . .

After a while she said, "Give Kennie a colt, Rob."

"He doesn't deserve it." The answer was short. Rob pushed away his papers and took out his pipe.

"Howard's too far ahead of him, older and bigger and quicker, and his wits about him, and——"

"Ken doesn't half try, doesn't stick at anything."

She put down her sewing. "He's crazy for a colt of his own. He hasn't had another idea in his head since you gave Highboy to Howard."

"I don't believe in bribing children to do their duty."

"Not a bribe." She hesitated.

"No? What would you call it?"

She tried to think it out. "I just have the feeling Ken isn't going to pull anything off, and"—her eyes sought Rob's "it's time he did. It isn't the school marks alone, but I just don't want things to go on any longer with Ken never coming out at the right end of anything."

"I'm beginning to think he's just dumb."

"He's not dumb. Maybe a little thing like this—if he had a colt of his own, trained him, rode him——"

Rob interrupted. "But it isn't a little thing, nor an easy thing, to break and school a colt the way Howard has schooled Highboy. I'm not going to have a good horse spoiled by Ken's careless ways. He goes woolgathering. He never knows what he's doing."

"But he'd *love* a colt of his own, Rob. If he could do it, it might make a big difference in him."

*"If* he could do it! But that's a big if."

At breakfast next morning Kennie's father said to him, "When you've done your study come out to the barn. I'm going in the car up to section twenty-one this morning to look over the brood mares. You can go with me."

"Can I go, too, Dad?" cried Howard.

McLaughlin frowned at Howard. "You turned Highboy out last evening with dirty legs."

Howard wriggled. "I groomed him——"

"Yes, down to his knees."

"He kicks."

"And whose fault is that? You don't get on his back again until I see his legs clean."

The two boys eyed each other, Kennie secretly triumphant and Howard chagrined. McLaughlin turned at the door, "And, Ken, a week from today I'll give you a colt. Between now and then you can decide what one you want."

Kennie shot out of his chair and stared at his father. "A—a spring colt, Dad, or a yearling?"

McLaughlin was somewhat taken aback, but his wife concealed a smile. If Kennie got a yearling colt he would be even up with Howard.

"A yearling colt, your father means, Ken," she said smoothly. "Now hurry with your lessons. Howard will wipe."

Kennie found himself the most important personage on the ranch. Prestige lifted his head, gave him an inch more of height and a bold stare, and made him feel different all the way through. Even Gus and Tim Murphy, the ranch hands, were more interested in Kennie's choice of a colt than anything else.

Howard was fidgety with suspense. "Who'll you pick, Ken? Say—pick Doughboy, why don't you? Then when he grows up he'll be sort of twins with mine, in his name anyway. Doughboy, Highboy, see?"

The boys were sitting on the worn wooden step of the door which led from the tack room into the corral, busy with rags and polish, shining their bridles.

Ken looked at his brother with scorn. Doughboy would never have half of Highboy's speed.

"Lassie, then," suggested Howard. "She's black as ink, like mine, And she'll be fast——"

"Dad says Lassie'll never go over fifteen hands."

Nell McLaughlin saw the change in Kennie, and her hopes rose. He went to his books in the morning with determination and really studied. A new alertness took the place of the day-dreaming. Examples in arithmetic were neatly written out, and as she passed his door before breakfast she often heard the monotonous drone of his voice as he read his American history aloud.

Each night, when he kissed her, he flung his arms around her and held her fiercely for a moment, then, with a winsome and blissful smile into her eyes, turned away to bed.

He spent days inspecting the different bands of horses and colts. He sat for hours on the corral fence, very important, chewing straws. He rode off on one of the ponies for half the day, wandering through the mile-square pastures that ran down toward the Colorado border.

And when the week was up he announced his decision. "I'll take that yearling filly of Rocket's. The sorrel with the cream tail and mane."

His father looked at him in surprise. "The one that got tangled in the barbed wire? That's never been named?"

In a second all Kennie's new pride was gone. He hung his head defensively. "Yes."

"You've made a bad choice, son. You couldn't have picked a worse."

"She's fast, Dad. And Rocket's fast——"

"It's the worst line of horses I've got. There's never one amongst them with real sense. The mares are hellions and the stallions outlaws; they're untamable."

"I'll tame her."

Rob guffawed. "Not I, nor anyone, has ever been able to really tame any one of them."

Kennie's chest heaved.

"Better change your mind, Ken. You want a horse that'll be a real friend to you, don't you?"

"Yes." Kennie's voice was unsteady.

"Well, you'll never make a friend of that filly. She's all cut and scarred up already with tearing through barbed wire after that bitch of a mother of hers. No fence'll hold 'em——"

"I know," said Kennie, still more faintly.

"Change your mind?" asked Howard briskly.

"No."

Rob was grim and put out. He couldn't go back on his word. The boy had to have a reasonable amount of help in breaking and taming the filly, and he could envision precious hours, whole days, wasted in the struggle.

Nell McLaughlin despaired. Once again Ken seemed to have taken the wrong turn and was back where he had begun; stoical, silent, defensive.

But there was a difference that only Ken could know. The way he felt about his colt. The way his heart sang. The pride and joy that filled him so full that sometimes he hung his head so they wouldn't see it shining out of his eyes.

He had known from the very first that he would choose that particular yearling because he was in love with her.

The year before, he had been out working with Gus, the big Swedish ranch hand, on the irrigation ditch, when they had noticed Rocket standing in a gully on the hillside, quiet for once, and eying them cautiously.

"Ay bet she got a colt," said Gus, and they walked carefully up the draw. Rocket gave a wild snort, thrust her feet out, shook her head wickedly, then fled away. And as they reached the spot they saw standing there the wavering, pinkish colt, barely able to keep its feet. It gave a little squeak and started after its mother on crooked, wobbling legs.

"Yee whiz! Luk at de little *flicka!*" said Gus.

"What does *flicka* mean, Gus?"

"Swedish for little gurl, Ken."

Ken announced at supper, "You said she'd never been named. I've named her. Her name is Flicka."

The first thing to do was to get her in. She was running with a band of yearlings on the saddleback, cut with ravines and gullies, on section twenty.

They all went out after her, Ken, as owner, on old Rob Roy, the wisest horse on the ranch.

Ken was entranced to watch Flicka when the wild band of youngsters discovered that they were being pursued and took off across the mountain. Footing made no difference to her. She floated across the ravines, always two lengths ahead of the others. Her pink mane and tail whipped in the wind. Her long delicate legs had only to aim, it seemed, at a particular spot, for her to reach it and sail on. She seemed to Ken a fairy horse.

He sat motionless, just watching and holding Rob Roy in, when his father thundered past on Sultan and shouted, "Well, what's the matter? Why didn't you turn 'em?

Kennie woke up and galloped after.

Rob Roy brought in the whole band. The corral gates were closed, and an hour was spent shunting the ponies in and out and through the chutes, until Flicka was left alone in the small round corral in which the baby colts were branded. Gus drove the others away, out the gate, and up the saddleback.

But Flicka did not intend to be left. She hurled herself against the poles which walled the corral. She tried to jump them. They were seven feet high. She caught her front feet over the top rung, clung, scrambled, while Kennie held his breath for fear the slender legs would be caught between the bars and snapped. Her hold broke; she fell over backward, rolled, screamed, tore around the corral. Kennie had a sick feeling in the pit of his stomach, and his father looked disgusted.

One of the bars broke. She hurled herself again. Another went. She saw the opening and, as neatly as a dog crawls through a fence, inserted her head and forefeet, scrambled through, and fled away, bleeding in a dozen places.

As Gus was coming back, just about to close the gate to the upper range, the sorrel whipped through it, sailed across the road and ditch with her inimitable floating leap, and went up the side of the saddleback like a jack rabbit.

From way up the mountain Gus heard excited whinnies, as she joined the band he had just driven up, and the last he saw of them they were strung out along the crest running like deer.

"Yee whiz!" said Gus, and stood motionless and staring until the ponies had disappeared over the ridge. Then he closed the gate, remounted Rob Roy, and rode back to the corral.

Rob McLaughlin gave Kennie one more chance to change his mind. "Last chance, son. Better pick a horse that you have some hope of riding one day. I'd have got rid of this whole line of stock if they weren't so damned fast that I've had the fool idea that someday there might turn out one gentle one in the lot—and I'd have a race horse. But there's never been one so far, and it's not going to be Flicka."

"It's not going to be Flicka," chanted Howard.

"Perhaps she *might* be gentled," said Kennie; and Nell, watching, saw that although his lips quivered, there was fanatical determination in his eye.

"Ken," said Rob, "it's up to you. If you say you want her we'll get her. But she wouldn't be the first of that line to die rather than give in. They're beautiful and they're fast, but let me tell you this, young man, they're *loco!*"

Kennie flinched under his father's direct glance.

"If I go after her again I'll not give up whatever comes; understand what I mean by that?"

"Yes."

"What do you say?"

"I want her."

They brought her in again. They had better luck this time. She jumped over the Dutch half door of the stable and crashed inside. The men slammed the upper half of the door shut, and she was caught.

The rest of the band was driven away, and Kennie stood outside of the stable, listening to the wild hoofs beating, the screams, the crashes. His Flicka inside there! He was drenched with perspiration.

"We'll leave her to think it over," said Rob when dinnertime came. "Afterward we'll go up and feed and water her."

But when they went up afterward there was no Flicka in the barn. One of the windows, higher than the mangers, was broken.

The window opened onto a pasture an eighth of a mile square, fenced in barbed wire six feet high. Near the stable stood a wagonload of hay. When they went around the back of the stable to see where Flicka had hidden herself they found her between the stable and the hay wagon, eating.

At their approach she leaped away, then headed east across the pasture.

"If she's like her mother," said Rob, "she'll go right through the wire."

"Ay bet she'll go over," said Gus. "She yumps like a deer."

"No horse can jump that," said McLaughlin.

Kennie said nothing because he could not speak. It was, perhaps, the most terrible moment of his life. He watched Flicka racing toward the eastern wire.

A few yards from it she swerved, turned, and raced diagonally south.

"It turned her! It turned her!" cried Kennie, almost sobbing. It was the first sign of hope for Flicka. "Oh, Dad! She has got sense. She has! She has!"

Flicka turned again as she met the southern boundary of the pasture, again at the northern; she avoided the barn. Without abating anything of her whirlwind speed, following a precise, accurate calculation and turning each time on a dime, she investigated every possibility. Then, seeing that there was no hope, she raced south toward the range where she had spent her life, gathered herself, and shot into the air.

Each of the three men watching had the impulse to cover his eyes, and Kennie gave a sort of a howl of despair.

Twenty yards of fence came down with her as she hurled herself through. Caught on the upper strands, she turned a complete somersault, landing on her back, her four legs dragging the wires down on top of her, and tangling herself in them beyond hope of escape.

"Damn the wire!" cursed McLaughlin. "If I could afford decent fences . . ."

Kennie followed the men miserably as they walked to the filly. They stood in a circle watching, while she kicked and fought and thrashed until the wire was tightly wound and knotted about her, cutting, piercing, and tearing great three-cornered pieces of flesh and hide. At last she was unconscious, streams of blood running on her golden coat, and pools of crimson widening and spreading on the grass beneath her.

With the wire cutter which Gus always carried in the hip pocket on his overalls he cut all the wire away, and they drew her into the pasture, repaired the fence, placed hay, a box of oats, and a tub of water near her, and called it a day.

"I don't think she'll pull out of it," said McLaughlin.

Next morning Kennie was up at five, doing his lessons. At six he went out to Flicka.

She had not moved. Food and water were untouched. She was

no longer bleeding, but the wounds were swollen and caked over.

Kennie got a bucket of fresh water and poured it over her mouth. Then he leaped away, for Flicka came to life, scrambled up; got her balance, and stood swaying.

Kennie went a few feet away and sat down to watch her. When he went in to breakfast she had drunk deeply of the water and was mouthing the oats.

There began then a sort of recovery. She ate, drank, limped about the pasture, stood for hours with hanging head and weakly splayed-out legs, under the clump of cottonwood trees. The swollen wounds scabbed and began to heal.

Kennie lived in the pasture too. He followed her around; he talked to her. He, too, lay snoozing or sat under the cottonwoods; and often, coaxing her with hand outstretched, he walked very quietly toward her. But she would not let him come near her.

Often she stood with her head at the south fence, looking off to the mountain. It made the tears come to Kennie's eyes to see the way she longed to get away.

Still Rob said she wouldn't pull out of it. There was no use putting a halter on her. She had no strength.

One morning, as Ken came out of the house, Gus met him and said, "De filly's down."

Kennie ran to the pasture, Howard close behind him. The right hind leg which had been badly swollen at the knee joint had opened in a festering wound, and Flicka lay flat and motionless, with staring eyes.

"Don't you wish now you'd chosen Doughboy?" asked Howard.

"Go away!" shouted Ken.

Howard stood watching while Kennie sat down on the ground and took Flicka's head on his lap. Though she was conscious and moved a little she did not struggle nor seem frightened. Tears rolled down Kennie's checks as he talked to her and petted her. After a few moments Howard walked away.

"Mother, what do you do for an infection when it's a horse?" asked Kennie.

"Just what you'd do if it was a person. Wet dressings. I'll help you, Ken. We mustn't let those wounds close or scab over until they're clean. I'll make a poultice for that hind leg and help you put it on. Now that she'll let us get close to her, we can help her a lot."

"The thing to do is see that she eats," said Rob. "Keep up her strength."

But he himself would not go near her. "She won't pull out of it," he said. "I don't want to see her or think about her."

Kennie and his mother nursed the filly. The big poultice was bandaged on the hind leg. It drew out much poisoned matter, and Flicka felt better and was able to stand again.

She watched for Kennie now and followed him like a dog, hopping on three legs, holding up the right hind leg with its huge knob of a bandage in comical fashion.

"Dad, Flicka's my friend now; she likes me," said Ken.

His father looked at him. "I'm glad of that, son. It's a fine thing to have a horse for a friend."

Kennie found a nicer place for her. In the lower pasture the brook ran over cool stones. There was a grassy bank, the size of a corral, almost on a level with the water. Here she could lie softly, eat grass, drink fresh running water. From the grass, a twenty-foot hill sloped up, crested with overhanging trees. She was enclosed, as it were, in a green, open-air nursery.

Kennie carried her oats morning and evening. She would watch for him to come, eyes and ears pointed to the hill. And one evening Ken, still some distance off, came to a stop and a wide grin spread over his face. He had hear her nicker. She had caught sight of him coming and was calling to him!

He placed the box of oats under her nose, and she ate while he stood beside her, his hand smoothing the satin-soft skin under her mane. It had a nap as deep as plush. He played with her long, cream-colored tresses, arranged her forelock neatly between her eyes. She was a bit dish-faced, like an Arab, with eyes set far apart. He lightly groomed and brushed her while she stood turning her head to him whichever way he went.

He spoiled her. Soon she would not step to the stream to drink but he must hold a bucket for her. And she would drink, then lift her dripping muzzle, rest it on the shoulder of his blue chambray shirt, her golden eyes dreaming off into the distance, then daintily dip her mouth and drink again.

When she turned her head to the south and pricked her ears and stood tense and listening, Ken knew she heard the other colts galloping on the upland.

"You'll go back there someday, Flicka," he whispered. "You'll be three, and I'll be eleven. You'll be so strong you won't know I'm on your back, and we'll fly like the wind. We'll stand on the very top where we can look over the whole world and smell the snow from the Neversummer Range. Maybe we'll see antelope. . . ."

This was the happiest month of Kennie's life.

With the morning Flicka always had new strength and would hop three-legged up the hill to stand broadside to the early sun, as horses love to do.

The moment Ken woke he'd go to the window and see her there, and when he was dressed and at his table studying he sat so that he could raise his head and see Flicka.

After breakfast she would be waiting at the gate for him and the box of oats, and for Nell McLaughlin with fresh bandages and buckets of disinfectant. All three would go together to the brook, Flicka hopping along ahead of them as if she were leading the way.

But Rob McLaughlin would not look at her.

One day all the wounds were swollen again. Presently they opened, one by one, and Kennie and his mother made more poultices.

Still the little filly climbed the hill in the early morning and ran about on three legs. Then she began to go down in flesh and almost overnight wasted away to nothing. Every rib showed; the glossy hide was dull and brittle and was pulled over the skeleton as if she were a dead horse.

Gus said, "It's de fever. It burns up her flesh. If you could stop de fever she might get vell."

McLaughlin was standing in his window one morning and saw the little skeleton hopping about three-legged in the sunshine, and he said, "That's the end. I won't have a thing like that on my place."

Kennie had to understand that Flicka had not been getting well all this time; she had been slowly dying.

"She still eats her oats," he said mechanically

They were all sorry for Ken. Nell McLaughlin stopped disinfecting and dressing the wounds. "It's no use, Ken," she said gently, "you know Flicka's going to die, don't you?"

"Yes, Mother."

Ken stopped eating. Howard said, "Ken doesn't eat anything any more. Don't he have to eat his dinner, Mother?"

But Nell answered, "Leave him alone."

Because the shooting of wounded animals is all in the day's work on the western plains, and sickening to everyone, Rob's voice, when he gave the order to have Flicka shot, was as flat as if he had been telling Gus to kill a chicken for dinner.

"Here's the Marlin, Gus. Pick out a time when Ken's not around and put the filly out of her misery."

Gus took the rifle. "*Ja,* boss. . . ."

Ever since Ken had known that Flicka was to be shot he had kept his eye on the rack which held the firearms. His father allowed no firearms in the bunkhouse. The gun rack was in the dining room of the ranch house, and going through it to the kitchen three times a day for meals, Ken's eye scanned the weapons to make sure that they were all there.

That night they were not all there. The Marlin rifle was missing.

When Kennie saw that he stopped walking. He felt dizzy. He kept staring at the gun rack, telling himself that it surely was there—he counted again and again—he couldn't see clearly. . . . Then he felt an arm across his shoulders and heard his father's voice.

"I know, son. Some things are awful hard to take. We just have to take 'em. I have to, too."

Kennie got hold of his father's hand and held on. It helped steady him.

Finally he looked up. Rob looked down and smiled at him and gave him a little shake and squeeze. Ken managed a smile too.

"All right now?"

"All right, Dad."

They walked in to supper together.

Ken even ate a little. But Nell looked thoughtfully at the ashen color of his face and at the little pulse that was beating in the side of his neck.

After supper he carried Flicka her oats but he had to coax her, and she would only eat a little. She stood with her head hanging but when he stroked it and talked to her she pressed her face into his chest and was content. He could feel the burning heat of her body. It didn't seem possible that anything so thin could be alive.

Presently Kennie saw Gus come into the pasture carrying the Marlin. When he saw Ken he changed his direction and sauntered along as if he was out to shoot some cottontails.

Ken ran to him. "When are you going to do it, Gus?"

"Ay was goin' down soon now, before it got dark. . . ."

"Gus, don't do it tonight. Wait till morning. Just one more night, Gus."

"Vell, in de morning den, but it got to be done, Ken. Yer fader gives de order."

"I know. I won't say anything more."

An hour after the family had gone to bed Ken got up and put on his clothes. It was a warm moonlit night. He ran down to the brook, calling softly. "Flicka! Flicka!"

But Flicka did not answer with a little nicker; and she was not in the nursery nor hopping about the pasture. Ken hunted for an hour.

At last he found her down the creek, lying in the water. Her head had been on the bank, but as she lay there the current of the stream had sucked and pulled at her, and she had had no strength to resist; and little by little her head had slipped down until when Ken got there only the muzzle was resting on the bank, and the body and legs were swinging in the stream.

Kennie slid into the water, sitting on the bank, and he hauled at her head. But she was heavy, and the current dragged like a weight; and he began to sob because he had no strength to draw her out.

Then he found a leverage for his heels against some rocks in the bed of the stream and he braced himself against these and pulled with all his might; and her head came up onto his knees, and he held it cradled in his arms.

He was glad that she had died of her own accord, in the cool water, under the moon, instead of being shot by Gus. Then, putting his face close to hers, and looking searchingly into her eyes, he saw that she was alive and looking back at him.

And then he burst out crying and hugged her and said, "Oh, my little Flicka, my little Flicka."

The long night passed.

The moon slid slowly across the heavens.

The water rippled over Kennie's legs and over Flicka's body. And gradually the heat and fever went out of her. And the cool running water washed and washed her wounds.

When Gus went down in the morning with the rifle they hadn't moved. There they were, Kennie sitting in water over his thighs and hips, with Flicka's head in his arms.

Gus seized Flicka by the head and hauled her out on the grassy bank and then, seeing that Kennie couldn't move, cold and stiff and half-paralyzed as he was, lifted him in his arms and carried him to the house.

"Gus," said Ken through chattering teeth, "don't shoot her, Gus."

"It ain't fur me to say, Ken. You know dat."

"But the fever's left her, Gus."

"Ay wait a little, Ken. . . ."

Rob McLaughlin drove to Laramie to get the doctor, for Ken was in violent chills that would not stop. His mother had him in bed wrapped in hot blankets when they got back.

He looked at his father imploringly as the doctor shook down the thermometer.

"She might get well now, Dad. The fever's left her. It went out of her when the moon went down."

"All right, son. Don't worry. Gus'll feed her, morning and night, as long as she's——"

"As long as I can't do it," finished Kennie happily.

The doctor put the thermometer in his mouth and told him to keep it shut.

All day Gus went about his work, thinking of Flicka. He had not been back to look at her. He had been given no more orders. If she was alive the order to shoot her was still in effect. But Kennie was ill, McLaughlin making his second trip to town taking the doctor home, and would not be back till long after dark.

After their supper in the bunkhouse Gus and Tim walked down to the brook. They did not speak as they approached the filly, lying stretched out flat on the grassy bank, but their eyes were straining at her to see if she was dead or alive.

She raised her head as they reached her.

"By the powers!" exclaimed Tim. "There she is!"

She dropped her head, raised it again, and moved her legs and became tense as if struggling to rise. But to do so she must use her right hind leg to brace herself against the earth. That was the damaged leg, and at the first bit of pressure with it she gave up and fell back.

"We'll swing her onto the other side," said Tim. "Then she can help herself."

"*Ja. . . .*"

Standing behind her, they leaned over, grabbed hold of her left legs, front and back, and gently hauled her over. Flicka was as lax and willing as a puppy. But the moment she found herself lying on her right side, she began to scramble, braced herself with her good left leg, and tried to rise.

"Yee whiz!" said Gus. "She got plenty strength yet."

"Hi!" cheered Tim. "She's up!"

But Flicka wavered, slid down again, and lay flat. This time she gave notice that she would not try again by heaving a deep sigh and closing her eyes.

Gus took his pipe out of his mouth and thought it over. Orders or no orders, he would try to save the filly. Ken had gone too far to be let down.

"Ay'm goin' to rig a blanket sling fur her, Tim, and get her on her feet, and keep her up."

There was bright moonlight to work by. They brought down the posthole digger and set two aspen poles deep into the ground either side of the filly, then, with ropes attached to the blanket, hoisted her by a pulley.

Not at all disconcerted, she rested comfortably in the blanket under her belly, touched her feet on the ground, and reached for the bucket of water Gus held for her.

Kennie was sick a long time. He nearly died. But Flicka picked up. Every day Gus passed the word to Nell, who carried it to Ken. "She's cleaning up her oats." "She's out of the sling." "She bears a little weight on the bad leg."

Tim declared it was a real miracle. They argued about it, eating their supper.

"Na," said Gus. "It was de cold water, washin' de fever outa her. And more dan dat—it was Ken—you tink it don't count? All night dot boy sits dere and says, 'Hold on, Flicka, Ay'm here wid you. Ay'm standin' by, two of us togedder'. . . ."

Tim stared as Gus without answering, while he thought it over. In the silence a coyote yapped far off on the plains, and the wind made a rushing sound high up in the jack pines on the hill.

Gus filled his pipe.

"Sure," said Tim finally. "Sure. That's it."

Then came the day when Rob McLaughlin stood smiling at the foot of Kennie's bed and said, "Listen! Hear your friend?"

Ken listened and heard Flicka's high, eager whinny.

"She don't spend much time by the brook any more. She's up at the gate of the corral half the time, nickering for you."

"For me!"

Rob wrapped a blanket around the boy and carried him out to the corral gate.

Kennie gazed at Flicka. There was a look of marveling in his eyes. He felt as if he had been living in a world where everything was dreadful and hurting but awfully real; and *this* couldn't be real; this was all soft and happy, nothing to struggle over or worry about or fight for any more. Even his father was proud of him! He could feel it in the way Rob's big arms held him. It was all like a dream and far away. He couldn't, yet, get close to anything.

But Flicka—Flicka—alive, well, pressing up to him, recognizing him, nickering . . .

Kennie put out a hand—weak and white—and laid it on her face. His thin little fingers straightened her forelock the way he used to do, while Rob looked at the two with a strange expression about his mouth and a glow in his eyes that was not often there.

"She's still poor, Dad, but she's on four legs now."

"She's picking up."

Ken turned his face up, suddenly remembering. "Dad! She did get gentled, didn't she?"

"Gentle—as a kitten. . . ."

They put a cot down by the brook for Ken, and boy and filly got well together.

# The End of the Race

*from* ALCATRAZ, THE WILD STALLION

*by Max Brand*

*I hope that by including the last two chapters of* Alcatraz *by Max Brand (Frederick Faust), I won't spoil reading the book for you. It is a great and touching story in its entirety and a first-rate example of a Max Brand Western.*

*The author, who was killed in action on the Italian front in 1944, was a most prolific writer, having thirty million words to his credit. From 1917 to 1941, he averaged a novel every three weeks.*

*Frederick Faust used numerous pseudonyms; Max Brand for Westerns, and others in such diverse fields as the far north, detective, romance, secret service, humor, and adventure. His work appeared in countless magazines, from pulp to* Harper's. *Reputedly his rate of pay for pulps was the highest anyone ever received. He was such an intriguing character that he is the subject of two biographies,* The Fabulous Faust Fanzine *and* Max Brand: The Man And His Work.

God A'mighty," said Red Perris, "I sure ain't done much to make You listen to me, but I got this to say: that if they's a call for something to die right now it ain't the hoss that's to blame. It's me that hounded him into the river.

Alcatraz ain't any pet, but he's sure lived according to his rights. Let him live and I'll let him go free. I got no right to him. I didn't make him. I never owned him. But let him stand up on his four legs again; let me see him go galloping once more, the finest hoss that ever bucked a fool man out of the saddle, and I'll call it quits!"

It was near to a prayer, if indeed this were not a prayer in truth. And glancing down to the head on his lap, he shivered with superstitious wonder. Alcatraz had unquestionably drawn a long and sighing breath.

The recovery was no miracle. The strangling coil of rope which shut off the wind of Alcatraz had also kept any water from passing into his lungs, and as the air now began to come back and the reviving oxygen reached his blood, his recovery was amazingly rapid. Before Perris had ceased wondering at the first audible breath the eyes of Alcatraz were lighted with flickering intelligence; then a snort of terror showed that he realized his nearness to the Great Enemy. His very panic acted as a thrillingly powerful restorative. By the time Perris got weakly to his feet, Alcatraz was lunging up the river bank scattering gravel and small rocks behind him.

And Perris made no attempt to throw the rope again. He allowed it to lie limp and wet on the gravel, but turning to watch that magnificent body, shining from the river, he saw the lines of Hervey's hunters coming swinging across the plain, riding to the limit of the speed of their horses.

This was the end, then. In ten minutes, or less, they would be on him, and he without a gun in his hands!

As though he saw the same approaching line of riders, Alcatraz whirled on the edge of the sand, but he did not turn to flee. Instead, he lifted his head and turned his bright eyes on the Great Enemy, and stood there trembling at their nearness! The heart of Perris leaped. A great hope which he dared not frame in thought rushed through his mind, and he stepped slowly forward, his hand extended, his voice caressing. The chestnut winced one step back, and then waited, snorting. There he waited, trembling with fear, chained by curiosity, and ready to leap away in arrowy flight should the sun wink on the tell-tale brightness of steel or the noosed rope dart whispering through the air above him. But there was no such sign of danger. The man came steadily on with his right hand stretched out palm up in the age-old token of amity, and as he approached he kept talking. Strange power was in that voice to enter the ears of the stallion and find a way to his heart of hearts. The fierce and joyous battle-note which he had heard on the day of the great fight was gone and in its place was a fiber of piercing gentleness. It thrilled Alcatraz as the touch of the man's fingers had thrilled him on another day.

Now he was very near, yet Perris did not hurry, did not change the quiet of his words. By the nearness his face was become the dominant thing. What was there between the mountains so terrible and so gentle, so full of awe, of wisdom, and of beauty, as this human face? Behind the eyes the outlaw horse saw the workings of that mystery which had haunted his still evenings in the desert—the mind.

Far away the gray mare was neighing plaintively and the scared cowpony trailed in the distance wondering why these free creatures should come so close to man, the enslaver; but to Alcatraz the herd was no more than a growth of trees; nothing existed under the sky saving that hand ceaselessly outstretched towards him, and the steady murmur of the voice.

He began to wonder: what would happen if he waited until the finger tips were within a hair's-breadth of his nose? Surely there would be no danger, for even if the Great Enemy slid onto his back again he could not stay, weak as Red Perris now was.

Alcatraz winced, but without moving his feet; and when he straightened the finger tips touched the velvet of his nose. He stamped and snorted to frighten the hunter away but the hand moved dauntlessly high and higher—it rested between his eyes—it passed across his head, always with that faint tingle of pleasure trailing behind the touch; and the voice was saying in broken tones: "Some damn fools say they ain't a God! Some damn fools! Something for nothing. That's what He gives! Steady, boy: steady!"

Between perfect fear and perfect pleasure, the stallion shuddered. Now the Great Enemy was beside him with a hand slipping down his neck. Why did he not swerve and race away? What power chained him to the place? He jerked his head about and caught the shoulder of Perris in his teeth. He could crush through muscles and sinews and smash the bone. But the teeth of Alcatraz did not close for the hunter made no sign of fear or pain.

"You're considerable of an idiot, Alcatraz, but you don't know no better," the voice was saying. "That's right, let go that hold. In the old days I'd of had my rope on you quicker'n a wink. But what good in that? The hoss I love ain't a down-headed, mean-hearted man-killer like you used to be; it's the Alcatraz that I've seen running free here in the Valley of the Eagles. And if you come with me, you come free and you stay free. I don't want to set no brand on you. If you stay it's because you like me, boy; and when you want to leave the corral gate will be sure open. Are you coming along?"

The fingers of that gentle hand had tangled in the mane of Alcatraz, drawing him softly forward. He braced his feet, snorting, his ears back. Instantly the pressure on his mane ceased. Alcatraz stepped forward.

"By God," breathed the man. "It's true! Alcatraz, old hoss, d'you think I'd ever of tried to make a slave out of you if I'd guessed that I could make you a partner?"

Behind them, the rattle of volleying hoofs was sweeping closer. The rain had ceased. The air was a perfect calm, and the very grunt of the racing horses was faintly audible, and the cursing of the men as they urged their mounts forward. Towards that approaching fear, Alcatraz turned his head. They came as though they would run him into the river. But what did it all mean? So long as one man stood beside him, he was shielded from the enmity of all other men. That had been true even in the regime of the dastardly Cordova.

"Steady!" gasped Red Perris. "They're coming like bullets, Alcatraz, old timer! Steady!"

One hand rested on the withers, the other on the back of the chestnut, and he raised himself gingerly up. Under the weight the stallion shrank catwise, aside and down. But there was no wrench of a curb in his mouth, no biting of the cinches. In the old days of his colthood, a barelegged boy used to come into the pasture and jump on his bare back. His mind flashed back to that—the bare, brown legs. That was before he had learned that men ride with leather and steel. He waited, holding himself strongly on leash, ready to turn loose his whole assortment of tricks—but Perris slipped into place almost as lightly as that dimly remembered boy in the pasture.

To the side, that line of rushing riders was yelling and waving hats. And now the light winked and glimmered on naked guns.

"Go!" whispered Perris at his ear. "Alcatraz!"

And the flat of his hand slapped the stallion on the flank. Was not that the old signal out of the pasture days, calling for a gallop?

He started into a swinging canter. And a faint, half-choked cry of pleasure from the lips of his rider tingled in his ears. For your born horseman reads his horse by the first buoyant moment, and what Red Jim Perris read of the stallion surpassed his fondest dreams. A yell of wonder rose from Hervey and his charging troop. They had seen Red Jim come battered and exhausted from his struggle with the stallion the day before, and now he sat upon the bareback of the chestnut—a miracle!

"Shoot!" yelled Hervey. "Shoot for the man. You can't hit the damned hoss!"

In answer, a volley blazed, but what they had seen was too

much for the nerves of even those hardy hunters and expert shots. The volley sang about the ears of Perris, but he was unscathed, while he felt Alcatraz gather beneath him and sweep into a racing pace, his ears flat, his neck extended. For he knew the meaning of that crashing fire. Fool that he had been not to guess. He who had battled with him the day before, but battled without man's ordinary tools of torture; he who had saved him this very day from certain death in the water; this fellow of the flaming red hair, was in truth so different from other men, that they hunted him, they hated him, and therefore they were sending their waspish and invisible messengers of death after him. For his own safety, for the life of the man on his back, Alcatraz gave up his full speed.

And Perris bowed low along the stallion's neck and cheered him on. It was incredible, this thing that was happening. They had reached top speed, and yet the speed still increased. The chestnut seemed to settle towards the earth as his stride lengthened. He was not galloping. He was pouring himself over the ground with an endless succession of smooth impulses. The wind of that running became a gale. The blown mane of Alcatraz whipped and cut at the face of Perris, and still the chestnut drove swifter and swifter.

He was cutting down the bank of the river which had nearly seen his death a few moments before, striving to slip past the left flank of Hervey's men, and now the foreman, yelling his orders, changed his line of battle, and the cowpunchers swung to the left to drive Alcatraz into the very river. The change of direction unsettled their aim. It is hard at best to shoot from the back of a running horse at an object in swift motion; it is next to impossible when sharp orders are being rattled forth. They fired as they galloped, but their shots flew wild.

In the meantime, they were closing the gap between them and the river bank to shut off Alcatraz, but for every foot they covered the chestnut covered two, it seemed. He drove like a red lightning bolt, with the rider flattened on his back, shaking his fist back at the pursuers.

"Pull up!" shouted Lew Hervey, in sudden realization that Alcatraz would slip through the trap. "Pull up! And shoot for Perris! Pull up!"

They obeyed, wrenching their horses to a halt, and as they drew them up, Red Jim, with a yell of triumph, straightened on the back of the flying horse and waved back to them. The next instant his shout of defiance was cut short by the bark of three rifles, as Hervey and Shorty and Little Joe, having halted their horses, pitched their guns to their shoulders and let blaze after the fugitive. There was a sting along the shoulder of Perris as though a red hot knife had slashed him; a bullet had grazed the skin.

Ah, but they would have a hard target to strike, from now on! The trick which Alcatraz had learned in his own flights from the hunters he now brought back into play. He began to swerve from side to side as he raced.

Another volley roared from the cursing cow-punchers behind them, but every bullet flew wide as the chestnut swerved.

"Damn him!" yelled Lew Hervey. "Has the hoss put the charm on the hide of that skunk, too?"

For in the fleeing form of Red Perris he saw all his hopes eluding his grasp. With Red Jim escaped and his promise to the rancher unfulfilled, what would become of his permanent hold on Oliver Jordan? Ay, and Red Jim, once more in safety and mounted on that matchless horse, would swoop down on the Valley of the Eagles and strike to kill, again, again, and again!

No wonder there was an agony shrill in the voice of the foreman as he shouted: "Once more!"

Up went the shining barrels of the rifles, followed the swerving form of the horseman for a moment, and then, steadied to straight, gleaming lines, they fired at the same instant, as though in obedience to an unspoken order.

And the form of Red Perris was knocked forward on the back of Alcatraz!

Some place in his body one of those bullets had struck. They saw him slide far to one side. They saw, while they shouted in triumph, that Alcatraz instinctively shortened his pace to keep his slipping burden from falling.

"He's done!" yelled Hervey, and shoving his rifle back in its holster, he spurred again in the pursuit.

But Red Perris was not done. Scrambling with his legs, tugging with his arms, he drew himself into position and straightway collapsed along the back of Alcatraz with both hands interwoven in the mane of the horse.

And the stallion endured it! A shout of amazement burst from the foreman and his men. Alcatraz had tossed up his head, sent a ringing neigh of defiance floating behind him, and then struck again into his matchless, smooth flowing gallop!

Perhaps it was not so astonishing, after all, as some men could have testified who have seen horses that are devils under spur and saddle become lambs when the steel and the leather they have learned to dread are cast away.

But all Alcatraz could understand, as his mind grasped vaguely towards the meaning of the strange affair, was that the strong, agile power on his back had been suddenly destroyed. Red Perris was now a limp and hanging weight, something no longer to be feared, something to be treated, at will, with contempt. The very voice was changed and husky as it called to him, close to his ear. And he no longer dared to dodge, because at every swerve that limp burden slid far to one side and dragged itself back with groans of agony. Then something warm trickled down over his shoulder. He turned his head. From the breast of the rider a crimson trickle was running down over the chestnut hair, and it was blood. With the horror of it he shuddered.

He must gallop gently, now, at a sufficient distance to keep the rifles from speaking behind him, but slowly and softly enough to keep the rider in his place. He swung towards the mares, running, frightened by the turmoil, in the distance. But a hand on his neck pressed him back in a different direction and down into the trail which led, eventually, to the ranch of Oliver Jordan. Let it be, then, as the man wished. He had known how to save a horse from the Little Smoky. He would be wise enough to keep them both safe even from other men, and so, along the trail towards the ranch, the chestnut ran with a gait as gentle as the swing and light fall of a ground swell in mid-ocean.

Far behind him he could see the pursuers driving their horses at a killing gallop. He answered their spurt and held them safely in the distance with the very slightest of efforts. All his care was given to picking out the easiest way, and avoiding jutting rocks and sharp turns which might unsettle the rider. Just as, in those dim old days in the pasture, when the short brown legs of the boy could not encompass him enough to gain a secure grip, he used to halt gently, and turn gently, for fear of unseating the urchin. How far more cautious was his maneuvering now! Here on his back was the power which had saved him from the river. Here on his back was he whose trailing fingers had given him his first caress.

He had no power of reason in his poor blind brain to teach him the why and the wherefore. But he had that overmastering impulse which lives in every gentle-blooded horse—the great desire to serve. A mustang would have been incapable of such a thing, but in Alcatraz flowed the pure strain of the thoroughbred, tracing back to the old desert stock where the horse lives in the tent of his master, the most cherished member of the family. There was in him dim knowledge of events through which he himself had never passed. By the very lines of his blood there was bred in him a need for human affection and human care, just as there was bred in him the keen heart of the racer. And now he knew to the full that exquisite delight of service with the very life of a helpless man given into his keeping.

One ear he canted back to the pain-roughened voice which spoke at his ear. The voice was growing weaker and weaker, just as the grip of the legs was decreasing, and the hands were tangled less firmly in his mane, but now the bright-colored buildings of the ranch appeared through the trees. They were passing between the deadly rows of barbed wire with far-off mutter of the pursuing horses beating at his ear and telling him that all escape was cut off. Yet still the man held him to the way through a mingling of trails thick with the scents of man, of man-ridden horses. The burden on his back now slipped from side to side at every reach of his springy gallop.

They came in sight of the ranch house itself. The failing voice rose for one instant into a hoarse cry of joy. Far behind, rose a triumphant echo of shouting. Yes, the trap was closed, and his only protection from the men riding behind was this half-living creature on his back.

Out from the arched entrance to the patio ran a girl. She started back against the 'dobe wall of the house and threw up one hand as though a miracle had flashed across her vision. Alcatraz brought his canter to a trot that shook the loose body on his back, and then he was walking reluctantly forward, for towards the girl the rider was directing him against all his own power of reason. She was crying out, now, in a shrill voice, and presently through the shadowy arch swung the figure of a big man on crutches, who shouted even as the girl had shouted.

Oliver Jordan, reading through the lines of his foreman's letter, had returned to find out what was going wrong, and from his daughter's tale he had learned more than enough.

Trembling at the nearness of these two human beings, but driven on by the faint voice, and the guiding hands, Alcatraz passed shuddering under the very arch of the patio entrance and so found himself once more—and forever—surrendered into the power of men!

But the weak figure on his back had relaxed, and was sliding down. He saw the gate closing the patio swing to. He saw the girl run with a cry and receive the bleeding body of Red Perris into her arms. He saw the man on crutches swing towards them, exclaiming "—without even a bridle! Marianne, he must have hypnotized that hoss!"

"Oh, Dad," the girl wailed, "if he dies—if he dies——"

The eyes of Perris, where he lay on the flagging, opened wearily.

"I'll live—I can't die! But Alcatraz . . . keep him from butcher Hervey . . . keep him safe. . . ."

Then his gaze fixed on the face of Oliver Jordan and his eyes widened in amazement.

"My father," she said, as she cut away the shirt to get at the wound.

"Him!" muttered Perris.

"Partner," said Oliver Jordan, wavering above the wounded man on his crutches, "what's done is done."

"Ay," said Perris, smiling weakly, "if you're her father that trail is sure ended. Marianne—get hold of my hand—I'm going out again . . . keep Alcatraz safe. . . ."

His eyes closed in a faint.

Between the cook and Marianne they managed to carry the limp figure to the shelter of the arcade just as Hervey and his men thundered up to the closed gate of the patio, and there the foreman drew rein in a cloud of dust and cursed his surprise at the sight of the ranchman.

The group in the patio, and the shining form of Alcatraz, were self explanatory. His plans were ruined at the very verge of a triumph. He hardly needed to hear the voice of Jordan saying: "I asked you to get rid of a gun-fighting killer—and you've tried to murder a *man*. Hervey, get out of the Valley and stay out if you're fond of a whole skin!"

And Hervey went.

. . . . . . .

There followed a strange time for Alcatraz. He could not be led from the patio. They could only take him by tying every hoof and dragging him, and such force Marianne would not let the cowpunchers use. So day after day he roamed in that strange corral while men came and stared at him through the strong bars of the gate, but no one dared enter the enclosure with the wild horse saving the girl alone, and even she could not touch him.

It was all very strange. And strangest of all was when the girl came out of the door through which the master had been carried and looked at Alcatraz, and wept. Every evening she came but she had no way of answering the anxious whinny with which he called for Red Jim again.

Strange, too, was the hush which brooded over the house. Even the cowpunchers, when they came to the gate, talked softly. But still the master did not come. Two weeks dragged on, weary weeks of waiting, and then the door to the house opened and again they carried him out on a wicker couch, a pale and wasted figure, around whom the man on the crutches and the girl and half a dozen cowpunchers gathered laughing and talking all at once.

"Stand back from him, now," ordered Marianne, "and watch Alcatraz."

So they drew away under the arcade and Alcatraz heard the voice of the master calling weakly.

It was not well that the others should be so near. For how could one tell from what hand a rope might be thrown or in what hand a gun might suddenly flash? But still the voice called and Alcatraz went slowly, snorting his protest and suspicion, until he stood at the foot of the couch and stretching forth his nose, still with his frightened glance fixed on the watchers, Alcatraz sniffed the hand of Red Jim. It turned. It patted him gently. It drew his gaze away from the others and into the eyes of this one man, the mysterious eyes which understood so much.

"A lone trail is right enough for a while, old boy," Red Jim was saying, "but in the end we need partners, a man and a woman and a horse and a man."

And Alcatraz, feeling the trail of the finger tips across the velvet skin of his muzzle, agreed.

# Jim McNab's Story

*from* MIDNIGHT

*by Sam Savitt*

*When one speaks of "rodeo greats," the name Midnight always comes to mind. In Jim McNab's story from* Midnight, *Sam Savitt tells with feeling the tale of a talented horse who by "going wrong" earned fame for himself and fortune for his masters.*

*Sam Savitt, like his hero Will James, writes and illustrates his own stories, but unlike James, Savitt is better known for his drawings and paintings of horses in action than for his writing.*

*Probably the outstanding illustrator of horse books in this country and responsible for the jacket of this volume, Sam Savitt lives with his wife, Bette, and two teen-age youngsters at One Horse Farm in Westchester County, New York.*

*He is an experienced horseman, and whenever he can escape from his studio, he rides, hunts, and works with young horses.*

Yes sir, I knew that Midnight horse from the very beginning. Of course his name wasn't Midnight then, we just called him that big black colt, and he came down from the hills one spring with a bunch of other fuzzies all ready to be made into a good working cow horse. He was a four-year-old, been saddle broke the summer before with the rest of his young buddies, and we had no reason to believe he wouldn't go straight to work with very few shenanigans. I'd been away to the war and was real anxious to get back in the saddle.

The gate of the corral was wide open and as the last one thundered through the opening, I swung it shut. 'Round and 'round they went with the dust so thick you could hardly see the hand in front of your face. They sure were a spooky bunch, been turned out all winter and I guess the unfenced freedom had gone to their heads. When they finally bunched at the far end of the corral and the atmosphere cleared a bit, I noticed this black one. And black he was, black as midnight, with a devil-may care look to go with it—and proud too. What a picture he made—head high, long black mane blowing wild, eyes flashing fire! I think what really caught my attention were his eyes—they were dark with that "look of eagles," and right then and there I got a hankering for him which I never got over.

"Okay, boys, this one's mine!" My loop snaked out and when it settled around his powerful neck he stood perfectly still—waiting. I approached him hand over hand along the rope—when I was about six feet away I stopped and looked him over. He was a well-made horse with maybe a strain of thoroughbred and a dash of Percheron, a little too long in the barrel, but put together real solid-like—stood about fifteen one and I figured about thirteen hundred pounds strong.

Seems like it only happened yesterday—it was a day like any other for that time of year, sunny with just the right amount of coolness in the air. I felt real good, no sense of foreboding, no nothing.

The saddle was cinched up—one of my boys had a good tight hold on his halter and I grinned and said, "Here goes nothing!" as I swung aboard. Now remember, so far this bronc hadn't made a wrong move—just stood there, steady, braced—later that was one of the things everyone remembered about Midnight—

he never wasted energy—just waited until it was time. And the time had come, right now! I never knew what hit me. Something slammed me from underneath—twisted my back sideways—jammed my face into the dirt, and then I was sitting on the ground looking up at him. This couldn't be true—no horse ever piled me that easily. Maybe I'd gotten a little rusty in the war, sorta lost my feel—"Hold him boys, let's try it again!"

Well . . . after the third try I just sat there on the ground awhile and thought things over. Hank, one of my ranch hands, cautiously joined me and we both sat there smoking cigarettes and watching the wrangler and his crew round up Midnight a fourth time—snag him with ropes from both sides, and jerk off saddle and halter.

"Looks like we got ourselves a bucking horse, boss," says Hank finally.

"Looks like," I grunted, "we've got the top bucking horse in the whole wide world—right now he knows more tricks, and packs more power, than any horse I ever rode. Man he's murder!"

Yes sir, that's the way it all began—on a nice spring day back in the year 1919—on my cottonwood ranch in southern Alberta.

I had the reputation of being a pretty fair bronc buster and before long word got around that old Jim McNab had got his comeuppance—he'd been rolled in the dust by one black horse—three times in a row. From miles around ranch hands came, most of 'em to look and admire, a few to try their luck at riding the Midnight horse. Their luck was always rotten.

Up to this point I still couldn't get it through my noggin that Midnight would never make a working cow horse. I liked this bronc, I liked the way he moved, I liked his quick intelligent eye, and most of all I liked his heart. Here was a horse who would never say die—guess it was the thoroughbred in him. Here was a horse whose friendship was worth cultivating. I figured he needed a new beginning, a fresh start, and I proceeded to try to give it to him.

I spent long hours just standing out there in the corral talking to him—saying lots of sweet nothings—and finally I could run my hand over his neck and sort of pull his mane playful-like. Sometimes I gently rubbed the velvet of his warm muzzle, and when I scratched the curlicue of hair on his forehead he would half close his eyes in a sleepy way. And sometimes I put my cheek against the side of his neck and smelled the warm sweetness of him. It was sorta like walking through a field of new mown hay with warm sun on your face. Before long, he nickered and came to meet me when I went into the pasture, then followed me around like a big black dog. He was a challenge to me but he was the kind of horse you couldn't rush into anything. I figured the slow easy way was the best way with Midnight—and now when I look back I believe I was right, because those were real happy days all filled with promise. As the months passed a strong bond of understanding grew between us.

One bright morning I slipped a bit into his mouth and he took it easier than I expected him to. I led him around the corral encouraging him with quiet words and soft cowboy ballads. We were getting there. Be gentle, be kind—it was bound to pay off. He looked a bit worried when I showed him a saddle, but after he smelled it very thoroughly and made sure it wasn't going to bite, he let me put in on his back. More walking—more talking—saddle off, saddle on—maybe three, four days of this. And then one afternoon I got on—after the saddle. He jigged a bit and for one moment I thought, here he goes! But he settled down and walked out—and the day looked brighter.

Then came Twenty-one Johnson—you probably never heard of him. He was a shrewd one, that gent. Had himself calluses, too, from patting his own back. His racket was riding wild horses for a suitable wager and then investing his profits in sky-limit blackjack games. Johnson had a gimmick—he used a saddle with an eighteen-inch swell—when he pressed his powerful thighs against that broad swell no horse alive could shake him loose. Anyway, that's what Twenty-one boasted—and he backed his claim with fifty dollars.

I recognized him one late afternoon when he was better than a mile off. You couldn't miss the dazzling white shirt, and nobody but Twenty-one Johnson displayed black sideburns that protruded about half a foot from each side of his face. I watched him drive through the front gate, long and lank, and all pretzeled up in the front seat of his buckboard with his saddle right behind him. "Hi-ya, Twenty-one—come to make a little money?"

He nodded, climbed down, hitched up his belt, and said, "Where's that Midnight horse? His day has come!"—and maybe it had. The boys started gathering then—grinning, winking at each other.

Midnight was brought out, head high against a taut halter shank, lights jumping all over his sleek blackness, proud, defiant—yet almost casual.

Hank had him snubbed down while Twenty-one slid his saddle on, drew himself up and in. "All set Johnson boy? Got those legs in close—good hold on that shank? Okay, Hank, let 'er rip!"

Down came Midnight's head and up went Midnight. So powerful, so urgent was his thrust that great clumps of sod followed him, and as he rolled at the top of his arc, his quarters twisted and shot skyward. Then the earth exploded and blurred and as Midnight came into focus again, I could see Johnson was still with him, but I could also see that he wasn't doing too well. He had blown both stirrups, had a strangle hold on his saddle horn, and his head was bobbing like a jack-in-the-box. They were going up for the third time now—Twenty-one's eyes were glazing fast—a big chunk of daylight leaped in between him and the saddle, and as Midnight dropped the curtain for the third time Johnson was on his way. Spread-eagled and spiraling out of the sun, he slammed the ground with such impact that it took about twenty minutes and two buckets of water to make him realize that he had just lost himself fifty bucks—and his reputation.

After that slick exhibition I couldn't resist giving Midnight a whirl with the best riders in Canada. Little did I know then that I was launching one of the greatest bucking horses in rodeo history. I signed him up for the bucking horse events in the local stampede at McCleod. Two riders got him in the draw.

Rodeo rules require a rider to stay in the saddle ten seconds, using only one rein which cannot be knotted or wrapped around the wrist. He must ride with one hand in the air, and can't change hands on the rein. He must come out raking his spurs fore and aft. He is disqualified if thrown, if he pulls leather, that is, grabs the saddle horn, or if he "blows" a stirrup. Applying rosin to the seat of the pants is barred.

The first rider hit the airways in four seconds. The second man made a mistake. He gouged my black horse with his spurs —the first spurs Midnight had ever felt driven home in deadly earnest—and that was it! Before this it had been a game—you try to stay on, I try to buck you off—but when those spurs hit . . . WOW! He squealed and twisted in the middle of a straight buck, ears flat back, mouth wide open, nostrils flaring red—you'd think he was some giant serpent dragon from medieval times. The viciousness, which up to now played beneath the surface, burst outward. When his front feet struck earth, up came that head, leaving the man balanced against a flapping rein. As he shot skyward again his rider followed the original course—straight down!

Two seconds! That was all!—and the crowd was on its feet! Here was a four-footed explosion, here was a powerhouse with the disposition of a buzz saw—an outlaw—a manhater. Here was a horse to be reckoned with.

After the McCleod stampede we took Midnight back to the ranch. Hank went on up to the bunkhouse and I turned the black horse into the corral and stood leaning my elbows on the top rail, watching him move about the enclosure. There was an awful sinking feeling in the pit of my stomach. I had made a mistake. Even before I walked up to him I knew it was no use—that something between us was gone now. He backed off, watching me suspiciously. When I held out my hand and spoke, he snorted and wheeled making a half-circle to the far end of the corral where he stood, head high, with too much white showing in the eye. I knew then the damage had been done. There was no turning back, no second chance, and a great sadness came over me, an emptiness which left an ache in my throat that wouldn't swallow.

Well, several weeks went by or maybe months—I don't remember now, but I couldn't get that Midnight horse off my mind. I couldn't shake the depression that dogged me wherever I went or whatever I did. I guess I was becoming a little hard to live with and maybe a little hard to work for, too. I'd say to myself, "Jim, this is no way for a grown man to act. You can't let a horse get you down like this—it's plumb foolishness. Now, buck up man, and forget it." But somehow I couldn't forget it.

Then a new situation came up which didn't help my disposition one bit. Some of the top riders from the big Red Deer outfit challenged me to enter Midnight in the Calgary Stampede—the biggest rodeo in Canada. They wanted a crack at my "wonder horse." I refused to accept their challenge, but when the Red Deer straw boss claimed I was afraid to risk my bucking horse against "good riders" I blew my stack.

Midnight was entered, and on the opening day of the Calgary Stampede I sat in the stands, miserable and remorseful, and cussing my wild pride for being taken. A black premonition sat beside me—a strange kind of fright shook my insides and made my teeth chatter, for I felt that before this day was through I would lose my Midnight horse forever.

Red Deer's top bronc rider drew Midnight first. He settled

into the saddle with grinning confidence. "Get in there real tight boy!"—"Don't let him throw you now."—"Let's show that black devil who's boss!"

Midnight was steady as a rock, no fuss, no wasted motion. Chute number eight—the gate swung wide and for one breathless instant nothing happened. Then Midnight erupted into the light—a black tornado against a sunny sky, then smoking earthward with a whip-snapping shock that brought the blood spurting from his rider's nostrils. Three in a row like that and the man came clear—as if shot out of a gun into the earth. The roaring stands went silent in hushed horror, as Midnight turned and approached the unconscious rider. It's hard to say what a horse will do sometimes, and for one frightening moment I thought the worst was going to happen. Instead, he nuzzled the fallen rider, and as the pickup men broke from their trance and rushed toward the prostrate figure, Midnight carefully stepped over the man and trotted toward the exit. His job was done, there was no sense in rubbing it in. The stadium thundered with spontaneous applause—the spectators had just witnessed a top-rate performance. They knew they had seen a great bucking horse in action, and their hearts went out to him. Midnight had found his destiny in the swirling dust of the arena, and I realized then he was lost to me forever. I sat there with my head in my hands.

Yep, six days the Stampede lasted, and in that time Midnight blasted every man who tried to ride him. Each victory gave him more confidence, and by the time the rodeo wound up, he was going like a dynamo and getting better each time he came out. Upon his final victory he was proclaimed the champion bucking horse of Western Canada.

He came home in a blaze of glory, but I knew he was hopelessly beyond my reach. Seeing him every day at the ranch and knowing he would never be the cow horse I had hoped for was more than I could stand. So—I decided to sell him, never thought I could, but I did.

Animals have a funny way of sensing things. Somehow they seem to know what you're going to do before you do it. Maybe it's because we telegraph our feelings and thoughts in a hundred and one ways we are completely unaware of—I don't know. But I'm sure Midnight knew I had come to this decision. Out in the pasture he seemed to keep to himself and often I'd see him standing alone, his head high, testing the wind and a distant far-away look in his eye. Sometimes I walked out there, and now he'd let me come right up to him again and put my hand on his withers, my face against his neck, and he'd bring his head around and nicker softly. He knew we were coming to the end of the line and I wondered if in some way he felt the same yearning, the same regrets I did.

Calgary promoter Peter Welch became Midnight's proud new owner. He came for him on a cold wet afternoon, and I remember thinking, this day looks like I feel. There were several horses in the corral and as usual of late, Midnight was standing apart. He raised his head and watched me approach. When the others moved off he waited. He seemed resigned and a little sad, too. This was the parting of the ways. I think he understood, and at that moment a kinship arose between us which had been dead these many months. As I brought the halter up he dropped his head to meet it, and when I fastened the buckle I was looking into his warm dark eye and my vision blurred, and a cold chill shook my shoulders. I turned with the lead rope in my hand and he followed me out quietly. I couldn't look at him—there was a great weariness inside me, and then I handed the halter shank to Welch.

"Be good to him, Pete, he's a great one." I almost choked on the words. I turned away—my hands sunk deep in the pockets of my Mackinaw, my shoulders hunched against the raw wind. I heard Midnight go up the ramp—I heard the tail gate snap shut—the motor catch and accelerate, and as the van rattled down the drive part of me went with it. I turned then and I was standing alone. The world was gray and empty, like my heart.

# RACING

# My Old Man

## *by Ernest Hemingway*

*No sporting anthology would be complete without "My Old Man," Ernest Hemingway's sole contribution to racing literature. In* A Moveable Feast, *sketches of the author's life in Paris in the twenties published in 1964, Hemingway mentions that this outstanding character study of a down-at-heel jockey was one of the two stories saved when his wife's suitcase, containing most of his early work, was stolen at the Gare de Lyon railroad station.*

*Written by the greatest master of the modern short story, "My Old Man" was first published by Contact Publishing Company in Paris in 1923. This little-known concern cautiously printed three hundred copies, any one of which would be worth a great deal of money today. It was not until 1925 that the publishing house of Charles Scribner's Sons took note of the young expatriate and included "My Old Man" in a collection entitled* In Our Time.

I guess looking at it, now, my old man was cut out for a fat guy, one of those regular little roly fat guys you see around, but he sure never got that way, except a little toward the last, and then it wasn't his fault, he was riding over the jumps only and he could afford to carry plenty of weight then. I remember the way he'd pull on a rubber shirt over a couple of jerseys and a big sweat shirt over that, and get me to run with him in the forenoon in the hot sun. He'd have, maybe, taken a trial trip with one of Razzo's skins early in the morning after just getting in from Torino at four o'clock in the morning and beating it out to the stables in a cab and then with the dew all over everything and the sun just staring to get going, I'd help him pull off his boots and he'd get into a pair of sneakers and all these sweaters and we'd start out.

"Come on, kid," he'd say, stepping up and down on his toes in front of the jock's dressing room, "let's get moving."

Then we'd start off jogging around the infield once, maybe, with him ahead, running nice, and then turn out the gate and along one of those roads with all the trees along both sides of them that run out from San Siro. I'd go ahead of him when we hit the road and I could run pretty good and I'd look around and he'd be jogging easy just behind me and after a little while I'd look around again and he'd begun to sweat. Sweating heavy and he'd just be dogging it along with his eyes on my back, but when he'd catch me looking at him he'd grin and say, "Sweating plenty?" When my old man grinned, nobody could help but grin too. We'd keep right on running out toward the mountains and then my old man would yell, "Hey, Joe!" and I'd look back and he'd be sitting under a tree with a towel he'd had around his waist wrapped around his neck.

I'd come back and sit down beside him and he'd pull a rope out of his pocket and start skipping rope out in the sun with the sweat pouring off his face and him skipping rope out in the white dust with the rope going cloppetty, cloppetty, clop, clop, clop, and the sun hotter, and him working harder up and down a patch of the road. Say, it was a treat to see my old man skip rope, too. He could whirr it fast or lop it slow and fancy. Say, you ought to have seen wops look at us sometimes, when they'd come by, going into town walking along with big white steers hauling the cart. They sure looked as though they thought the old man was nuts. He'd start the rope whirring till they'd stop dead still and watch him, then give the steers a cluck and a poke with the goad and get going again.

When I'd sit watching him working out in the hot sun I sure felt fond of him. He sure was fun and he done his work so hard and he'd finish up with a regular whirring that'd drive the sweat out on his face like water and then sling the rope at the tree and come over and sit down with me and lean back against the tree with the towel and a sweater wrapped around his neck.

"Sure is hell keeping it down, Joe," he'd say and lean back and shut his eyes and breathe long and deep, "it ain't like when you're a kid." Then he'd get up and before he started to cool we'd jog along back to the stables. That's the way it was keeping down to weight. He was worried all the time. Most jocks can just about ride off all they want to. A jock loses about a kilo every time he rides, but my old man was sort of dried out and he couldn't keep down his kilos without all that running.

I remember once at San Siro, Regoli, a little wop, that was riding for Buzoni, came out across the paddock going to the bar for something cool; and flicking his boots with his whip, after he'd just weighed in and my old man has just weighed in too, and came out with the saddle under his arm looking red-faced and tired and too big for his silks and he stood there looking at young Regoli standing up to the outdoors bar, cool and kid-looking, and I said, "What's the matter, Dad?" cause I thought maybe Regoli had bumped him or something and he just looked at Regoli and said, "Oh, to hell with it," and went on to the dressing room.

Well, it would have been all right, maybe, if we'd stayed in Milan and ridden at Milan and Torino, 'cause if there ever were any easy courses, it's those two. "Pianola, Joe," my old man said when he dismounted in the winning stall after what the wops thought was a hell of steeplechase. I asked him once. "This course rides itself. It's the pace you're going at, that makes riding the jumps dangerous, Joe. We ain't going any pace here, and they ain't really bad jumps either. But it's the pace always—not the jumps—that makes the trouble."

San Siro was the swellest course I'd ever seen but the old man said it was a dog's life. Going back and forth between Mirafiore and San Siro and riding just about every day in the week with a train ride every other night.

I was nuts about the horses, too. There's something about it, when they come out and go up the track to the post. Sort of dancy and tight looking with the jock keeping a tight hold on them and maybe easing off a little and letting them run a little going up. Then once they were at the barrier it got me worse than anything. Especially at San Siro with that big green infield and the mountains way off and the fat wop starter with his big whip and the jocks fiddling them around and then the barrier snapping up and that bell going off and them all getting off in a bunch and then commencing to string out. You know the way a bunch of skins gets off. If you're up in the stand with a pair of glasses all you see is them plunging off and then that bell goes off and it seems like it rings for a thousand years and then they come sweeping round the turn. There wasn't ever anything like it for me.

But my old man said one day, in the dressing room, when he was getting into his street clothes, "None of these things are horses, Joe. They'd kill that bunch of skates for their hides and hoofs up at Paris." That was the day he'd won the Premio Commercio with Lantorna shooting her out of the field the last hundred meters like pulling a cork out of a bottle.

It was right after the Premio Commercio that we pulled out and left Italy. My old man and Holbrook and a fat wop in a straw hat that kept wiping his face with a handkerchief were having an argument at a table in the Galleria. They were all talking French and the two of them was after my old man about something. Finally he didn't say anything any more but just sat there and looked at Holbrook, and the two of them kept after him, first one talking and then the other, and the fat wop always butting in on Holbrook.

"You go out and buy me a *Sportsman,* will you, Joe?" my old man said, and handed me a couple of soldi without looking away from Holbrook.

So I went out of the Galleria and walked over to in front of the Scala and bought a paper, and came back and stood a little way away because I didn't want to butt in and my old man was sitting back in his chair looking down at his coffee and fooling with a spoon and Holbrook and the big wop were standing and the big wop was wiping his face and shaking his head. And I came up and my old man acted just as though the two of them weren't standing there and said, "Want an ice, Joe?" Holbrook looked down at my old man and said slow and careful, "You son of a bitch," and he and the fat wop went out through the tables.

My old man sat there and sort of smiled at me, but his face was white and he looked sick as hell and I was scared and felt sick inside because I knew something had happened and I didn't see how anybody could call my old man a son of a bitch, and get away with it. My old man opened up the *Sportsman* and studied the handicaps for a while and then he said, "You got to take a lot of things in this world, Joe." And three days later we left Milan for good on the Turin train for Paris, after an auction sale out in front of Turner's stables of everything we couldn't get into a trunk and a suit case.

We got into Paris early in the morning in a long, dirty station the old man told me was the Gare de Lyon. Paris was an awful big town after Milan. Seems like in Milan, every boy is going somewhere and all the trams run somewhere and there ain't any sort of a mix-up, but Paris is all balled up and they never do straighten it out. I got to like it, though, part of it, anyway, and say, it's got the best race courses in the world. Seems as though that were the thing that keeps it all going and about the only thing you can figure on is that every day the buses will be going out to whatever track they're running at, going right out through everything to the track. I never really got to know Paris well, because I just came in about once or twice a week with the old man from Maisons and he always sat at the Café de la Paix on the Opera side with the rest of the gang from Maisons and I guess that's one of the busiest parts of the town. But, say, it is funny that a big town like Paris wouldn't have a Galleria, isn't it?

Well, we went out to live at Maisons-Lafitte, where just about everybody lives except the gang at Chantilly, with a Mrs. Meyers that runs a boarding house. Maisons is about the swellest place to live I've ever seen in all my life. The town ain't so much, but there's a lake and a swell forest that we used to go off bumming in all day, a couple of us kids, and my old man made me a sling shot and we got a lot of things with it but the best one was a magpie. Young Dick Atkinson shot a rabbit with it one day and we put it under a tree and were all sitting around and Dick had some cigarettes and all of a sudden the rabbit jumped up and beat it into the brush and we chased it but we couldn't find it. Gee, we had fun at Maisons. Mrs. Meyers used to give me lunch in the morning and I'd be gone all day. I learned to talk French quick. It's an easy language.

As soon as we got to Maisons, my old man wrote to Milan for his license and he was pretty worried till it came. He used to sit around the Café de Paris in Maisons with the gang, there were lots of guys he'd known when he rode up at Paris, before the war, lived at Maisons, and there's a lot of time to sit around because the work around a racing stable, for the jocks, that is, is all cleaned up by nine o'clock in the morning. They take the first bunch of skins out to gallop them at 5.30 in the morning and they work the second lot at 8 o'clock. That means getting up early all right and going to bed early, too. If a jock's riding for somebody too, he can't go boozing around because the trainer always has an eye on him if he's a kid and if he ain't a kid he's always got an eye on himself. So mostly if a jock ain't working he sits around the Café de Paris with the gang and they can all sit around about two or three hours in front of some drink like a vermouth and seltz and they talk and tell stories and shoot pool and it's sort of like a club or the Galleria in Milan. Only it ain't really like the Galleria because there everybody is going by all the time and there's everybody around at the tables.

Well, my old man got his license all right. They sent it through to him without a word and he rode a couple of times. Amiens, up country and that sort of thing, but he didn't seem to get any engagement. Everybody liked him and whenever I'd come into the Café in the forenoon I'd find somebody drinking with him because my old man wasn't tight like most of these jockies that have got the first dollar they made riding at the World's Fair in St. Louis in nineteen ought four. That's what my old man would say when he'd kid George Burns. But it seemed like everybody steered clear of giving my old man any mounts.

We went out to wherever they were running every day with the car from Maisons and that was the most fun of all. I was glad when the horses came back from Deauville and the summer. Even though it meant no more bumming in the woods, 'cause then we'd ride to Enghien or Tremblay or St. Cloud and watch them from the trainers' and jockeys' stand. I sure learned about racing from going out with that gang and the fun of it was going every day.

I remember once out at St. Cloud. It was a big two hundred thousand franc race with seven entries and Kzar a big favorite. I went around to the paddock to see the horses with my old man and you never saw such horses. This Kzar is a great big yellow horse that looks like just nothing but run. I never saw such a horse. He was being led around the paddocks with his head down and when he went by me I felt all hollow inside he was so beautiful. There never was such a wonderful, lean, running built horse. And he went around the paddock putting his feet just so and quiet and careful and moving easy like he knew just what he had to do and not jerking and standing up on his legs and getting wild eyed like you see these selling platers with a shot of dope in them. The crowd was so thick I couldn't see him again except just his legs going by and some yellow and my old man started out through the crowd and I followed him over to the jocks' dressing room back in the trees and there was a big crowd around there, too, but the man at the door in a derby nodded to my old man and we got in and everybody was sitting around and getting dressed and pulling shirts over their heads and pulling boots on and it all smelled hot and sweaty and linimenty and outside was the crowd looking in.

The old man went over and sat down beside George Gardner that was getting into his pants and said, "What's the dope, George?" just in an ordinary tone of voice 'cause there ain't any use him feeling around because George either can tell him or he can't tell him.

"He won't win," George says very low, leaning over and buttoning the bottoms of his breeches.

"Who will?" my old man says, leaning over close so nobody can hear.

"Kircubbin," George says, "and if he does, save me a couple of tickets."

My old man says something in a regular voice to George and George says, "Don't ever bet on anything I tell you," kidding like, and we beat it out and through all the crowd that was looking in, over to the 100 franc mutuel machine. But I knew something big was up because George is Kzar's jockey. On the way he gets one of the yellow odd-sheets with the starting prices on and Kzar is only paying 5 to 10, Cefisidote is next at 3 to 1 and fifth down the list this Kircubbin at 8 to 1. My old man bets five thousand on Kircubbin to win and put on a thousand to place and we went around back of the grandstand to go up the stairs and get a place to watch the race.

We were jammed in tight and first a man in a long coat with a gray tall hat and a whip folded up in his hand came out and then one after another the horses, with the jocks up and a stable boy holding the bridle on each side and walking along, followed the old guy. That big yellow horse Kzar came first. He didn't look so big when you first looked at him until you saw the length of his legs and the whole way he's built and the way he moves. Gosh, I never saw such a horse. George Gardner was riding him and they moved along slow, back of the old guy in the gray tall hat that walked along like he was a ring master in a circus. Back of Kzar, moving along smooth and yellow in the sun, was a good looking black with a nice head with Tommy Archibald riding him; and after the black was a string of five more horses all moving along slow in a procession past the grandstand and the pesage. My old man said the black was Kircubbin and I took a good look at him and he was a nice-looking horse, all right, but nothing like Kzar.

Everybody cheered Kzar when he went by and he sure was one swell-looking horse. The procession of them went around on the other side past the pelouse and then back up to the near end of the course and the circus master had the stable boys turn them loose one after another so they could gallop by the stands on their way up to the post and let everybody have a good look at them. They weren't at the post hardly any time at all when the gong started and you could see them way off across the infield all in a bunch starting on the first swing like a lot of little toy horses. I was watching them through the glasses and Kzar was running well back, with one of the bays making the pace. They swept down and around and came pounding past and Kzar was way back when they passed us and this Kircubbin horse in front and going smooth. Gee, it's awful when they go by you and then you have to watch them go farther away and get smaller and smaller and then all bunched up on the turns and then come around towards into the stretch and you feel like swearing and goddamming worse and worse. Finally they made the last turn and came into the straightaway with this Kircubbin horse way out in front. Everybody was looking funny and saying "Kzar" in sort of a sick way and them pounding nearer down the stretch, and then something came out of the pack right into my glasses like a horse-headed yellow streak and everybody began to yell "Kzar" as though they were crazy. Kzar came on faster than I'd ever seen anything in my life and pulled up on Kircubbin that was going fast as any black horse could go with the jock flogging hell out of him with the gad and they were right dead neck and neck for a second but Kzar seemed going about twice as fast with those great jumps and that head out—but it was while they were neck and neck that they passed the winning post and when the numbers went up in the slots the first one was 2 and that meant that Kircubbin had won.

I felt all trembly and funny inside, and then we were all jammed in with the people going downstairs to stand in front of the board where they'd post what Kircubbin paid. Honest, watching the race I'd forgot how much my old man had bet on Kircubbin. I'd wanted Kzar to win so damned bad. But now it was all over it was swell to know we had the winner.

"Wasn't it a swell race, Dad?" I said to him.

He looked at me sort of funny with his derby on the back of his head. "George Gardner's a swell jockey, all right," he said. "It sure took a great jock to keep that Kzar horse from winning."

Of course I knew it was funny all the time. But my old man saying that right out like that sure took the kick all out of it for me and I didn't get the real kick back again ever, even when they posted the numbers upon the board and the bell rang to pay off and we saw that Kircubbin paid 67.50 for 10. All round people were saying, "Poor Kzar! Poor Kzar!" And I thought, I wish I were a jockey and could have rode him instead of that son of a bitch. And that was funny, thinking of George Gardner as a son of a bitch because I'd always liked him and besides he'd given us the winner, but I guess that's what he is, all right.

My old man had a big lot of money after that race and he took to coming to Paris oftener. If they raced at Tremblay he'd have them drop him in town on their way back to Maisons and he and I'd sit out in front of the Café de la Paix and watch the people go by. It's funny sitting here. There's streams of people going by and all sorts of guys come up and want to sell you things, and I loved to sit there with my old man. That was when we'd have the most fun. Guys would come by selling funny rabbits that jumped if you squeezed a bulb and they'd come up to us and my old man would kid with them. He could talk French just like English and all those kind of guys knew him 'cause you can aways tell a jockey—and then we always sat at the same table and they got used to seeing us there. There were guys selling matrimonial papers and girls selling rubber eggs that when you squeezed them a rooster came out of them and one old wormy-looking guy that went by with post-cards of Paris, showing them to everybody, and, of course, nobody ever bought any, and then he would come back and show the under side of the pack and they would all be smutty post-cards and lots of people would dig down and buy them.

Gee, I remember the funny people that used to go by. Girls around supper time looking for somebody to take them out to eat and they'd speak to my old man and he'd make some joke at them in French and they'd pat me on the head and go on. Once there was an American woman siting with her kid daughter at the next table to us and they were both eating ices and I kept looking at the girl and she was awfully good looking and I smiled at her and she smiled at me but that was all that ever came of it because I looked for her mother and her every day and I made up ways that I was going to speak to her and I wondered if I got to know her if her mother would let me take her out to Auteuil or

Tremblay but I never saw either of them again. Anyway, I guess it wouldn't have been any good, anyway, because looking back on it I remember the way I thought out would be best to speak to her was to say, "Pardon me, but perhaps I can give you a winner at Enghien today?" and, after all, maybe she would have thought I was a tout instead of really trying to give her a winner.

We'd sit at the Café de la Paix, my old man and me, and we had a big drag with the waiter because my old man drank whisky and it cost five francs, and that meant a good tip when the saucers were counted up. My old man was drinking more than I'd ever seen him, but he wasn't riding at all now and besides he said that whisky kept his weight down. But I noticed he was putting it on, all right, just the same. He'd busted away from his old gang out at Maisons and seemed to like just sitting around on the boulevard with me. But he was dropping money every day at the track. He'd feel sort of doleful after the last race, if he'd lost on the day, until we'd get to our table and he'd have his first whisky and then he'd be fine.

He'd be reading the *Paris-Sport* and he'd look over at me and say, "Where's your girl, Joe?" to kid me on account I had told him about the girl that day at the next table. And I'd get red, but I liked being kidded about her. It gave me a good feeling. "Keep your eye peeled for her, Joe," he'd say, "she'll be back."

He'd ask questions about things and some of the things I'd say he'd laugh. And then he'd get started talking about things. About riding down in Egypt, or at St. Moritz on the ice before my mother died, and about during the war when they had regular races down in the south of France without any purses, or betting or crowd or anything just to keep the breed up. Regular races with the jocks riding hell out of the horses. Gee, I could listen to my old man talk by the hour, especially when he'd had a couple of drinks. He'd tell me about when he was a boy in Kentucky and going coon hunting, and the old days in the States before everything went on the bum there. And he'd say, "Joe, when we've got a decent stake, you're going back there to the States and go to school."

"What've I got to go back there to go to school for when everything's on the bum there?" I'd ask him.

"That's different," he'd say and get the waiter over and pay the pile of saucers and we'd get a taxi to the Gare St. Lazare and get on the train out to Maisons.

One day at Auteuil, after a selling steeplechase, my old man bought in the winner for 30,000 francs. He had to bid a little to get him but the stable let the horse go finally and my old man had his permit and his colors in a week. Gee, I felt proud when my old man was an owner. He fixed it up for stable space with Charles Drake and cut out coming in to Paris, and started his running and sweating out again, and him and I were the whole stable gang. Our horse's name was Gilford, he was Irish bred and a nice, sweet jumper. My old man figured that training him and riding him, himself, he was a good investment. I was proud of everything and I thought Gilford was as good as Kzar. He was a good, solid jumper, a bay, with plenty of speed on the flat, if you asked him for it, and he was a nice-looking horse, too.

Gee, I was fond of him. The first time he started with my old man up, he finished third in a 2500 meter hurdle race and when my old man got off him, all sweating and happy in the place stall, and went in to weigh, I felt as proud of him as though it was the first race he'd ever placed in. You see, when a guy ain't been riding for a long time, you can't make yourself really believe that he has ever rode. The whole thing was different now, 'cause down in Milan, even big races never seemed to make any difference to my old man, if he won he wasn't ever excited or anything, and now it was so I couldn't hardly sleep the night before a race and I knew my old man was excited, too, even if he didn't show it. Riding for yourself makes an awful difference.

Second time Gilford and my old man started, was a rainy Sunday at Auteuil, in the Prix du Marat, a 4500 meter steeplechase. As soon as he'd gone out I beat it up in the stand with the new glasses my old man had bought for me to watch them. They started way over at the far end of the course and there was some trouble at the barrier. Something with goggle blinders on was making a great fuss and rearing around and busted the barrier once, but I could see my old man in our black jacket, with a white cross and a black cap, sitting up on Gilford, and patting him with his hand. Then they were off in a jump and out of sight behind the trees and the gong going for dear life and the pari-mutuel wickets rattling down. Gosh, I was so excited, I was afraid to look at them, but I fixed the glasses on the place where they would come out back of the trees and then out they came with the old black jacket going third and they all saiing over the jump like birds. Then they went out of sight again and then they came pounding out and down the hill and all going nice and sweet and easy and taking the fence smooth in a bunch, and moving away from us all solid. Looked as though you could walk across on their backs they were all so bunched and going so smooth. Then they bellied over the big double Bullfinch and something came down. I couldn't see who it was, but in a minute the horse was up and galloping free and the field, all bunched still, sweeping around the long left turn into the straightaway. They jumped the stone wall and came jammed down the stretch toward the big water-jump right in front of the stands. I saw them coming and hollered at my old man as he went by, and he was leading by about a length and riding way out, and light as a monkey, and they were racing for the water-jump. They took off over the big hedge of the water-jump in a pack and then there was a crash, and two horses pulled sideways out off it, and kept on going, and three other were piled up. I couldn't see my old man anywhere. One horse kneed himself up and the jock had hold of the bridle and mounted and went slamming on after the place money. The other horse was up and away by himself, jerking his head and galloping with the bridle rein hanging and the jock staggered over to one side of the track against the fence. Then Gilford rolled over to one side off my old man and got up and started to run on three legs with his front off hoof dangling and there was my old man laying there on the grass flat out with his face up and blood all over the side of his head. I ran down the stand and bumped into a jam of people and got to the rail and a cop grabbed me and held me and two big stretcher-bearers were going out after my old man and around on the other side of the course I saw three horses, strung way out, coming out of the trees and taking the jump.

My old man was dead when they brought him in and while a doctor was listening to his heart with a thing plugged in his ears, I heard a shot up the track that meant they'd killed Gilford. I lay down beside my old man, when they carried the stretcher into the hospital room, and hung onto the stretcher and cried and cried, and he looked so white and gone and so awfully dead, and I couldn't help feeling that if my old man was dead maybe they didn't need to have shot Gilford. His hoof might have got well. I don't know. I loved my old man so much.

Then a couple of guys came in and one of them patted me on the back and then went over and looked at my old man and then pulled a sheet off the cot and spread it over him; and the other was telephoning in French for them to send the ambulance to take him out to Maisons. And I couldn't stop crying, crying and choking, sort of, and George Gardner came in and sat down beside me on the floor and put his arm around me and says, "Come on, Joe, old boy. Get up and we'll go out and wait for the ambulance."

George and I went out to the gate and I was trying to stop bawling and George wiped off my face with his handkerchief and we were standing back a little ways while the crowd was going out of the gate and a couple of guys stopped near us while we were waiting for the crowd to get through the gate and one of them was counting a bunch of mutuel tickets and he said, "Well, Butler got his, all right."

The other guy said, "I don't give a good goddam if he did, the crook. He had it coming to him on the stuff he's pulled."

"I'll say he had," said the other guy, and tore the bunch of tickets in two.

And George Gardner looked at me to see if I'd heard and I had all right and he said, "Don't you listen to what those bums said, Joe. Your old man was one swell guy."

But I don't know. Seems like when they get started they don't leave a guy nothing.

# The Hammond

*from* THE LOOK OF EAGLES

*by John Taintor Foote*

*This is the last chapter from one of the finest horse stories ever written.*

*Horses, dogs, and fishing absorbed much of John Taintor Foote's time, but in turn his hobbies supplied the raw material for his best writing.*

*Among the most unforgettable American sporting fiction is his* Look of Eagles, *about a horse;* Dumb-Bell of Brookfield, *about a dog; and a fishing yarn known as "The Wedding Gift."*

*Mr. Foote, who started his professional career as a mediocre artist, soon switched to writing, and has many magazine articles, short stories, plays, and seventeen books to his credit.*

*During the closing years of his life, the author lived in California, where he wrote for the movies. He died in 1950.*

Now listen!" he said. "You just looked at the best two-year-old God ever put breath in!"

I took in this incredible information slowly. I exulted in it for a moment, and then came doubts.

"How do you know?" I demanded.

"How do I know!" exclaimed Blister. "It 'ud take me a week to tell you. Man, he can fly! He makes his first start tomorrow—in the Hammond. Old Man Sanford'll get in tonight. Come out 'n' see a real colt run."

My brain was whirling

"In the Hammond?" I gasped. "Does Mr. Sanford know all this?"

Blister gave me a slow, a thoughtful look.

"It sounds nutty," he said; "but I can't figger it no other way. As sure as you 'n' me are standin' here—he knowed it from the very first!"

Until I closed my eyes that night I wondered whether Blister's words were true. If so, what sort of judgment, instinct, intuition, had been used that day at Thistle Ridge? I gave it up at last and slept, to dream of a colt that suddenly grew raven wings and soared over the grand stand while I nodded wisely and said: "Of course—the birthright of eagles!"

I got to Blister's stalls at one o'clock next day, and found Mr. Sanford clothed in a new dignity hard to describe. Perhaps he had donned it with the remarkable flowered waistcoat he wore—or was it due to his flowing double-breasted coat, a sprightly blue in color and suggesting inevitably a leather trunk, dusty, attic-bound, which had yawned and spat it forth?

"Welcome, suh; thrice welcome!" he said to me. "I take the liberty of presuming that the pu'ple and white is honored with yoh best wishes today."

I assured him that from the bottom of my heart this was so. He wrung my hand again and took out a gold watch the size of a bun.

"Three hours moh," he said, "before our hopes are realized or shattered."

"You think the colt will win?" I inquired.

Mr. Sanford turned to the southwest. I followed his eyes and saw a bank of evil-looking clouds creeping slowly up the sky.

"I like our chances, suh," he told me; "but it will depend on those clouds yondeh. We want a fast track foh the little chap. He is a swallow. Mud would break his heart."

"She's fast enough now," said Blister, who had joined us; and Mr. Sanford nodded.

So for three hours I watched the sky prayerfully and saw it become more and more ominous. When the bugle called for the Hammond at last, Latonia was shut off from the rest of the world by an inverted inky cup, its sides shot now and then with lightning flashes. We seemed to be in a great vacuum. I found my lungs snatching for each breath, while my racing card grew limp as I clutched its spasmodically in a sweating hand.

I had seen fit to take a vital interest in the next few moments; but I glanced at faces all about me in the grand stand and found them strained and unnatural. Perhaps in the gloom they seemed whiter than they really were; perhaps my own nerves pricked my imagination until this packed humanity became one beating heart.

I do not think that this was so. The dramatic moment goes straight to the soul of a crowd, and this crowd was to see the Hammond staged in a breathless dark, with the lightning's flicker for an uncertain spotlight.

No rain would spoil our chances that day, for now, across the center field at the half-mile post, a mass of colors boiled at the barrier. The purple and white was somewhere in the shifting, surging line, borne by a swallow, so I had been told. Well, even so, the blue and gold was there likewise—and carried by what? Perhaps an eagle!

Suddenly a sigh—not the customary roar, but a deep intaking of the grand stand's breath—told me they were on the wing. I strained my eyes at the blurred mass of them, which seemed to move slowly in the distance as it reached the far turn of the back stretch. Then a flash of lightning came and my heart skipped a beat and sank.

They were divided into two unequal parts. One was a crowded, indistinguishable mass. The other, far ahead in unassailable isolation, was a single spot of bay with a splash of color clinging above.

A roar of "Postman!" shattered the quiet like a bombshell, for that splash of color was blue and gold. The favorite was making a runaway race of it. He was coming home to twenty thousand joyful backers, who screamed and screamed his name.

Until that moment I had been the victim of a dream. I had come to believe that the little old man, standing silent at my side, possessed an insight more than human. Now I had wakened. He was an old fool in a preposterous coat and waistcoat, and I looked at him and laughed a mirthless laugh. He was squinting slightly as he peered with his washed-out eyes into the distance. His face was placid; and as I noticed this I told myself that he was positively witless. Then he spoke.

"The bay colt is better than I thought," he said.

"True," I agreed bitterly, and noted, as the lightning flashed again, that the blue and gold was an amazing distance ahead of those struggling mediocre others.

"A pretty race," murmured Old Man Sanford; and now I thought him more than doddering—he was insane.

Some seconds passed in darkness, while the grand stand gave off a contented murmur. Then suddenly the murmur rose to a new note. It held fear and consternation in it. My eyes leaped up the track. The bay colt had rounded the curve into the stretch. He was coming down the straight like a bullet; but—miracle of miracles!—it was plain that he was not alone. . . .

In a flash it came to me: stride for stride, on the far side of him, one other had maintained a flight equal to his own. And then I went mad; for this other, unsuspected in the darkness until now, commenced to creep slowly, surely, into the lead. Above his stretching neck his colors nestled proudly. He was bringing the purple and white safe home to gold and glory.

Nearer and nearer he came, this small demon whose coat

matched the heavens, and so shot past us, with the great Postman—under the whip—two lengths behind him!

I remember executing a sort of bear dance, with Mr. Sanford infolded in my embrace. I desisted when a smothered voice informed me that my conduct was "unseemly, suh—most unseemly!"

A rush to the track followed, where we found Blister, quite pale, waiting with a blanket. Suddenly the grand stand, which had groaned once and become silent, broke into a roar that grew and grew.

"What is it?" I asked.

Blister whirled and stared at the figures on the timing board. I saw a look of awe come into his face.

"What is it?" I repeated. "Why are they cheering? Is it the time?"

"Oh, no!" said Blister with scornful sarcasm and a look of pity at my ignorance. "It ain't the time!" He nodded at the figures. "That's only the world's record fur the age 'n' distance."

And now there came, mincing back to us on slender, nervous legs, something wet and black and wonderful. It pawed and danced wildly in a growing ring of curious eyes.

Then, just above the grand stand, the inky cup of the sky was broken and there appeared the light of an unseen sun. It turned the piled white clouds in the break to marvels of rose and gold. They seemed like the ramparts of heaven, set there to guard from earthly eyes the abode of the immortals.

"Whoa, man! Whoa, hon!" said Blister, and covered the heaving sides.

As he heard Blister's voice and felt the touch of the blanket the colt grew quiet. His eyes became less fiery wild. He raised his head, with its dilated blood-red nostrils, and stared—not at the mortals standing reverently about him, but far beyond our gaze—through the lurid gap in the sky, straight into Valhalla.

I felt a hand on my arm.

"The look of eagles, suh!" said Old Man Sanford.

# The Race

*from* THE WILL TO WIN

*by Jane McIlvaine*

*This is the final chapter of the true story of Jay Trump, the first American bred, owned, and ridden horse to win the toughest jumping race in the world, the Grand National at Liverpool, England.*

*It is the story of a racing heritage, dauntless persistence, hard knocks, and the will to win. The author, a friend and neighbor of Tommy Smith, Jay Trump's amateur rider, writes an exciting story about a subject she knows intimately.*

*An accomplished fox hunter herself, Jane McIlvaine (Mrs. Nelson McClary) brings to life both the supreme excitement of victory as well as the hard work and drudgery of making a champion.*

The moment so long awaited became reality. A reality of shouting and pounding of hoofs. A wild shuffle in which the most carefully planned strategy tended to go by the boards.

Released finally, the horses raced in a bunch, a wild dash impossible to control. Then the leaders were at fence number one. A swishing noise as twenty or more rose simultaneously.

One went down. Ayala, the 1963 winner. For Stan Mellor, the friendly and able jockey who had ridden Frenchman's Cove to victory over Jay Trump at Kempton, it was a quick end to his journey.

Jay Trump was on the inside with the way clear. He took off, seemed to hang in the air, then completed the arc of his first leap over an Aintree fence.

Ahead lay twenty-nine of the biggest, stiffest fences on earth.

The biggest number there is! Tommy thought.

Going into the second fence he wondered if he'd ever get to the last.

Already the field had begun to string out, Phebu, Peacetown, Freddie, L'Empereur, and The Rip setting the pace.

Jay Trump was well behind the leaders, going at an even hunting canter, lying on the rail. Tommy could see the horses ahead vanish as they jumped, then the jockeys' caps as they set off along the straight. At each fence he steadied Jay Trump. The bay responded like a ladies' hunter, placing himself, jumping superbly, and coping with the drops like a seasoned performer.

Ronald's Boy fell at the third and Red Tide at the fourth.

Then they were over the fifth and Becher's was rising before them.

The small red pennant with the white B on it fluttered against the blue of the sky. The infield rail and the space opposite were a solid mass of humanity. Many had been there for hours, eating, drinking, reading the morning paper, and listening to transistor radios. On the right loomed the high scaffold where the movie cameras were mounted. A BBC truck raced the field on the inside. Policemen, ambulance men, and photographers stood at intervals.

On the railway embankment, the signals were set at *Danger!*

As the leaders approached the volume of sound became deafening. What John Hislop describes as "the traditional freezing silence, and appearance of misery with which the English elite are wont to take their pleasures" gave way to unrestrained cheering. As the leading horses soared up from take-off the sound of drumming hoofs swelled to include the hissing, grunting sounds of labored breathing and effort, the creak of leather, and the clanging of steel. The jockeys' exclamations and the swishing of spruce boughs added to the cacophony as the horses strained and stretched in the downward arc to meet the ground and vanish from the sight of those behind.

Phebu, the neat little mare from Shropshire who liked to be in front, jumped first, then Dark Venetian and Peacetown. Freddie followed boldly, his tongue lolling from his mouth. Suddenly the surflike roar of the crowd was penetrated by sharp fearful cries of warning. Spruce boughs rained down as horses hit the top. The arcing rainbow against the sky disintegrated into a flurry of legs, falling horses, and bright-clad figures hurtling across the path of the oncoming field.

Nedsmar began it, landing short and tipping onto his nose. Forgotten Dreams crashed onto the back of Sword Flash, who, in some miraculous manner, managed to stand up. Ruby Glen, Barleycroft, Sizzle-on, and Crobeg left their riders lying like bright-colored toys against the green turf.

To Tommy, Becher's was like diving into black water. Blind to what was happening on the far side, he could only hope that Jay Trump would land safe or instinctively have another jump left in him to clear a fallen horse.

Jay Trump took it close to the inside rail. For an instant he seemed to dwell in mid-air. Then the descent, like falling off a building into the battlefield at Balaklava. Horses struggling to their feet. Jockeys lying with their heads protected by their arms.

There was no awkwardness on landing or backward contortions on the part of his rider. The Yank landed clear of the chaos and kept on running.

At Canal Turn, Freddie made a superb leap that brought him up behind Phebu. In the jostling and scrimmaging that took place Tommy maneuvered Jay Trump toward the center. In order to make full use of his left-turning tendency and come about for the mass change of direction he drove him at the fence at a forty-five degree angle. Jay Trump did it just right, jumping himself from about fifteenth position to ninth.

Game little Phebu was still in front. Behind her came Freddie, Peacetown, L'Empereur, Rondetto, and Kapeno. The announcer had not mentioned Jay Trump. Yet he was jumping flawlessly, covering the ground with his powerful stride.

"I could see then that he was going very well," Fred Winter said and was aware of breathing for the first time since the start.

"I could not see a thing," Mrs. Stephenson said. "It was like swimming underwater."

At Valentine's, Groomsman went down (it was said that the Duque had paid three thousand dollars a fence to ride in the National).

Over the next three fences the race acquired a certain continuity. Peacetown and Phebu leading, Freddie coming up on the inside. Rondetto and L'Empereur, The Rip and Kapeno running well. Now the sound of hoofs against the turf, the clink of metal and creaking leather, the grunts and exclamations, the sense of sweat and strain and restrained effort achieved a kind of rhythm.

Relief at being safely past the preceding fences gave way to elation. Jay Trump was going very well, jumping cleanly and with the confidence of a proven Aintree horse. Momentarily Tommy was to experience the wonder and glory and intensive exhilaration that make steeplechasing worth-while.

Simultaneously a cheerful voice rang out, "Why, Tommy, fancy meeting you here! How are you going?" To his amazement he saw Willie Robinson alongside. His Lambourn neighbor threw him an impish grin. Urging his horse on past he called back over his shoulder. "Good-by, I'm going on now!"

By then they were across Melling Road and on the race

course. Any thought of further chatter was lost in the growing roar heralding their approach to the stands.

Meanwhile the number of loose horses had been growing. As wavering and unpredictable as Sunday drivers they posed the problem of whether to try and pass them or suffer behind them. Rather than force their mounts to additional effort, the majority elected to stay behind and see which way they would veer at the fences.

At the thirteenth it was obvious there was going to be grief.

The riderless Red Tide had been with them since the fourth fence. Now he chose to swerve directly across the path of the leaders. In the confusion that followed, several horses refused and brave little Phebu was brought down. Jay Trump was in a precarious position. Lacking room to maneuver he was forced to jump with the pack. From the air Tommy saw Phebu's jockey lying directly where Jay Trump must land or crash into the horses alongside.

Tommy thought he heard a sickening crunch. He looked back over his shoulder. The jockey lay motionless. He felt sick. (Jockey Jimmy Morrissey suffered a concussion, is now fully recovered.)

Another fence. Then The Chair, looming like a wall against the horizon.

Jay Trump quickened his stride. Just inside the wings and well back from the ditch he took off. There were sharp exclamations from those on the ground as his strong quarters thrust him upward. Every muscle strained. Then the great, graceful arc was completed. The years of slow, patient work had achieved the collection and ability, marking him as one of the world's great jumpers.

By now the bad ones had fallen, refused, or been pulled up. Most of the loose horses had headed for the barn—all but Red Tide, who crashed into the infield, and Phebu, dauntless and determined to maintain her lead.

The runners left in the race negotiated the water jump high, wide, handsome, and bold, leaving behind them a memory of beauty and rhythm as even and smooth and shining as their reflections in the water as they flew past the stands.

Rondetto, Peacetown, Freddie, Kapeno, and The Rip, in a fluid arc like that of a Skeaping pastel.

Jay Trump was twelfth.

Now they had to do it all over again.

Going out into the country for the second circuit it was the riderless Phebu on top. Then Rondetto, Peacetown, Freddie, Kapeno, L'Empereur, Pontin-Go, and The Rip.

The green was cut up. Gorse and sprigs of spruce and fir littered the course, knocked out of the fences or carried on a bandage or a boot and then flung off on the straight. The horses were showing signs of battle. Their heads were lower, their sides white with foam. The riders' faces looked pale and strained. There was no longer any repartee as they slogged into their fences, grimly seeking to hold their tiring horses together.

Past the "Go Well—Go Shell" sign high on the embankment they went.

At each fence the roar of the crowd rose and fell. Now and then the name of a horse or a jockey could be distinguished from the drumming surflike sound beating against the rider's ears. At the eighteenth, Leedsy went down. Tommy saw his lighthearted friend Willie on the ground. For one flashing instant he saw his face. The impish leprechaun look was gone. In its place was an expression of pain and anguish, as, desperately, he sought to protect his damaged body from the horses pouring over him.

At the nineteenth, the open ditch, Phebu held the lead, followed by Rondetto, Peacetown, L'Empereur, Freddie, Pontin-Go, The Rip, Kapeno, and Jay Trump.

At the twentieth, a horse's rump struck Jay Trump's shoulder. He staggered, lost a stride, and then went on.

The roar of the crowd on the embankment signaled the second approach to Becher's.

Again Becher's took its toll. Kapeno swerved, hit the great fence hard, failed to clear the drop, and was gone. Dave Dick rolled free, was up in a flash, and tried to recapture the horse. But Kapeno ducked away, ending the veteran jockey's thirteenth Grand National.

The flesh and blood and spirit of the race began to take shape.

Canal Turn. The crucial fence. Phebu, reins dangling, jumped and then ran off course. Pontin-Go came down, leaving jockey Lehane with fractured ribs. And Jay Trump made the leap of his life. Avoiding the fallen horse, he jumped at a sheer forty-five-degree angle. Going from ninth place he landed just inside the rail and up with the leaders.

For the first time since the race began, the name Jay Trump was heard in the stands. "Jay Trump, Jay Trump!" shouted the announcer. "The Yank is moving up!"

Suddenly there was hope.

With it came exhaustion, slowly and relentlessly, creeping over Tommy's arms and legs, causing a terrible breathlessness, and bringing on the fear that he might not be able to finish.

Jay Trump was doing most of the work now. He was running strongly. The pistonlike rhythm of his stride took him past The Rip and L'Empereur as though they were standing.

Rondetto had been going brilliantly. At the twenty-sixth fence, the plain and relatively uncomplicated fence following Valentine's, the little chestnut swerved directly in front of Jay Trump, hit the fence, somersaulted, and landed in a sprawling, bone-crushing spill. Jay Trump was about to take off. It was too late to change direction.

The bay saw Rondetto, saw he couldn't clear him. And in that instant all that Jay Trump was came into being—his left-turning tendency, his training as a huntsman's horse in which he learned to avoid hounds underfoot, the handiness acquired through the hours of dressage work, plus his own native intelligence and ability.

In mid-air he made a flying change—an above-the-ground

ballet, after four miles and twenty-five fences. It was a second of perfection, that second of time no one sees, something that today must be viewed on film to be believed.

Throwing his body left he landed safely, on the correct lead, avoiding by inches the tangle of legs and the fallen jockey.

Ahead stretched the track. A long ribbon of green. The pack, the moving phalanx of bright-colored backs, was gone. Only two horses remained in front.

The roar of the crowd had died. The noise of the stands was still too far away to be heard. It was like coming from a rocky, storm-churned channel into wide, calm waters.

The next instant Jay Trump was alongside Freddie, the favorite, and Peacetown, on the outside, was falling back.

Which horse had the more to give? Both jockeys, the one a professional, the other an amateur, and both riding their first Grand National. They glanced quickly at each other and each thought, "Let him move first."

Then they were across Melling Road. As they turned for home Freddie's jockey moved. Tommy moved to keep up with him.

Now they'd done with the hunt. Two fences from the finish, the racing began.

Never in Aintree's history had two horses been so perfectly matched. Both eight-year-old geldings. Both of the same fox-hunting background. Both belonging to sporting owners who had staked their all on this one race. Now they were destined to make this, perhaps the last Grand National, as legendary as any run before.

The noise from the stands, starting as a whisper above the sound of the wind and hoofs and labored breathing, became a growing roar.

The Yank and the Scot . . . Freddie . . . Jay Trump . . . the rest of the field nowhere . . .

On they came, head and head, stride for stride, two horses running for their lives, their jockeys riding like thunder.

The wind rushed at them and the turf was flung up like waves in their wake. Now the last fence. The air was loud with roaring and the running increased. There wasn't time to think, or to do. Only a sudden flashing sensation of impending disaster. Jay Trump was going too fast. He was not collected. He was going to meet the fence wrong. Seconds now and they'd be down.

Jay Trump dove straight into the wall of green. Boughs caught at his legs and fell to the ground. The reins slipped through Tommy's hands.

Then they were over. Not over but through. Because of the holes knocked in it from the previous day's racing the horse had survived. Miraculously Jay Trump was still on his feet. Furthermore he had earned a crucial length over the favorite, who jumped it properly, high over the sticks, hunter style.

A sensation of sureness, of glory, swept from horse to man. Tommy picked up the reins and Jay Trump's great heart came up into his hands.

Those on the ground heard him yell.

"Now!"

There was still the run-in. Four hundred and ninety-four seemingly endless yards. A long green roadway bounded by white. The stands coming closer. The noise growing. A hundred thousand voices screaming, "Jay Trump and Freddie . . . the Yank and the Scot!"

The pace set from Melling Road would have crushed most horses before this. Still they struggled, Freddie for Scotland, Jay Trump for America. Sides white with lather, fighting, straining with each stride.

Both jockeys felt their muscles numbing, their breath leaving them. Which one would win the duel, the experienced professional or the American amateur?

Freddie inched forward.

"Freddie . . . Freddie . . . !" screamed the stands. "Scotland's got it!"

In those distended nostrils, in the tongue swinging from the opened mouth by his girth, Tommy recognized the threat, saw the end of the hopes, the dreams. Through his mind flashed one all encompassing thought. To win!

He had Jay Trump on the rail now and his whip in his left hand to keep him running straight. In a flash he transferred it to his right hand.

Like a border collie the Scottish horse hung on, refusing to fall back. For a second the whip stayed uncertain. Then it struck.

It was a move born of desperation, and one that was almost fatal.

Jay Trump swerved. He changed feet. His tail began to go around. He spit out the bit and stopped running.

Was it possible in those final seconds following the race of his life that the bay horse remembered his aversion to being struck on the right side? Could he have associated the whip and the white rail at Aintree with the accident that had come so close to ending his life?

Fred Winter was frantic. He stood in front of the American flag waving his arms like a wild man.

"Put the whip away . . . put the whip away . . . !"

Mrs. Stephenson could not speak. Tears streamed down her face.

Kitty Smith clutched her mother's arm. "You don't know how much Tommy wanted to win!"

Margot's vision blurred. In her mind's eye she saw Harry Worcester and Crompton. Father and son fighting it out to the finish . . . "O but I do!" she choked. "I do, indeed."

In all great moments there is a tingling awareness of something beyond description, something sensed rather than seen. In those last seconds of the historic race, almost as though in response to the pleas and exhortations from the stands, Tommy realized his mistake. He put the whip away. With his hands and his heart and his heritage he began to ride.

Jay Trump's tail stopped moving. He stretched out his head, picked up the bit, and went back to running.

For one trembling instant Freddie clung. Then Jay Trump shot out and the Scottish hope, as gallant a horse as ever faced an Aintree fence, was done.

"The Yank's gonna do it!" screamed the surging stands.

A few more strides. And the winning post shot backward.

Jay Trump had done it!

# Everybody Loves Kelso

## *by Suzanne Wilding*

*It is not often that one or two names dominate a sport; in horse racing it's Man O'War and Kelso. The former has been immortalized in countless books and articles, but the latter, the biggest money winner of all time and the only horse to be named "Horse of the Year" for five successive seasons, has little other than news and picture stories to his credit.*

*In 1965, noting the lack of Kelso material suitable for reprinting,* The Reader's Digest *commissioned an original piece about the horse. After much fascinating research and many high-level conferences, the article was ready the same month that an eye injury forced the durable Kelso to retire. The* Digest *lost interest and the article was shelved. But Kelso has withstood the test of time. Five years later, no horse has come near to equaling his record nor to taking his place in the heart of the American racing public. A homely brown gelding who made up in ability what he lacked in beauty, Kelso definitely deserves a place in this book.*

When Kelso, the horse that had dominated U. S. racing since 1960, battled down the home stretch beating four-year-old Malicious in the Whitney Stakes last summer, there was a sudden, almost absolute silence. Then, as if acting on cue, 50,000 hands began to beat time to Kelso's flying strides. That this form of cadenced clapping should suddenly arise from the horse players of Saratoga was like a whole new dream come true. It lasted from the quarter pole all the way to the finish line and was the greatest expression of love ever heard on an American track.

"Make way for the horses! Make way!" yelled an official as the crowd of 23,360 fans spilled out into Saratoga's famous old course.

"What horses?" a little girl asked her father. "Are there others than Kelso?"

At this writing nine-year-old Kelso, who has earned more money than any other thoroughbred in the history of racing, is only $22,000 short of the $2,000,000 mark. His closest rival, Round Table, earned $1,749,869 while the great Man O'War grossed a mere $259,000. And besides all that, in 1965 Kelso, the millionaire now turned philanthropist, started to make personal appearances for equine charity—an all time first for any horse.

When Kelso isn't at the track he spends his time making personal appearances for the benefit of the Grayson Foundation for equine research in Louisville, Kentucky and for the New Bolton Center branch of the University of Pennsylvania Veterinary School.

If it had not been for the lenient decision of Lloyds of London, the famous British insurance firm that spared the life of his sire, Your Host, Kelso would never have been born to win 39 races and to break countless speed, distance, and cash records.

During the 1951 season at California's Santa Anita track, Your Host, winner of 13 races and a tidy $384,000, crashed into the rail and broke his shoulder. He was insured with Lloyds, but the policy read that the money could only be collected if the horse's injury warranted destroying him. When Your Host's owner realized that the horse would never race again, he turned him over to Lloyds. Dead, Your Host was worth $250,000.

Meanwhile hundreds of fans wrote the august insurance company begging them to spare the courageous horse. Lloyds paid off the claim and instead of shooting the thoroughbred they called in the best veterinarians and tried to rehabilitate the unfortunate horse. But the stallion's right foreleg was permanently deformed, and again Your Host faced the firing squad.

At this point fate took over. F. Wallis Armstrong, a horse fancier who had polio in his youth and who, consequently, had a soft spot in his heart for the cripple, bought Your Host for $140,000. Another man might not have done it, but Armstrong did. He knew that the thoroughbred would never race again, but his blood lines were good, and for breeding purposes an unsound foreleg would be no drawback. In due course Your Host was mated with Maid of Flight, a granddaughter of Man O'War, and in the spring of 1957 a colt was born at Mrs. Richard C. duPont's Woodstock Farm, Chesapeake City, Maryland. He was named Kelso, "Kelly" to his friends.

He wasn't much to begin with. Small, slab-sided, irascible, hard to handle, he developed habits of kicking his groom, of biting people, and of cribbing—gnawing any surface into which he could get his teeth. His color was a dirty brown, his rump slanted like a slalom run, his quarters were too straight, and his neck was set on wrong. Moreover, he showed a weakness in one hind leg.

As only the best thoroughbreds are kept for breeding, Mrs. duPont decided to have him gelded. "The unkindest cut of all" (as one writer put it) probably cost his stable $4,000,000 in stud fees. But many experts, including Carl Hanford, his trainer, feel that as a stallion Kelso would never have become the great running machine he is today.

For all his unprepossessing appearances, Kelso has what it takes: heart, a will to win, and a dazzling stride. Bill Brewer, veterinarian of the New York Racing Association, says that Kelso has the strongest heartbeat of any horse he has ever examined. Another veterinarian insists that Kelso's heart is much larger than that of the average race horse. And when he runs, covering the ground in great kangaroo-like leaps, the ugly duckling turns into a beautiful swan. To his owner, his entourage, and thousands of racing fans who look at him through rose-colored glasses he is beautiful even when standing still.

Kelso's climb started modestly enough. He raced twice as a two-year-old in 1959. He won his maiden race in Atlantic City: $1,900 in prize money and paid fourteen dollars to win. Never again would he earn as little or pay as much to the two dollar bettor.

Things began moving in 1960 when Mrs. duPont sent her string of thoroughbreds to Carl Hanford, member of a family long connected with the track.

"Kelso put me on the map," the Nebraskan readily admits, his face lighting up when he recalls the early days. "I knew he had something the minute he started to gallop," Hanford told me. "Race horses are like school kids. Occasionally you get a straight A student. If you do, you must make the work fun for him. Don't let him skip a grade because he's bright and then get him sour because you ask him to do more than he can."

Hanford worries about equine boredom and talks of training a horse mentally as well as physically. A thoroughbred's life is not altogether a happy one, he'll agree. Whether at Saratoga or Santa Anita the routine is always the same. Early in the morning the horse is exercised on the track, and after that he spends 23 out of every 24 hours cooped up in his stall. His job is to run as fast as he knows how, and being fit and tense is part of that bargain. No wonder most race horses are unhappy and on edge!

"A horse is able to absorb just so much" Hanford tells you.

"You must never overtrain him." Maybe not being overtrained plus the fact that he wasn't raced hard as a two-year-old account for Kelso's amazing durability. Most race horses are through by the time they are four or five. Kelso, at eight, is still beating horses half his age.

If he wasn't pushed he was given every encouragement. Top jockeys are hard to come by for an unproven thoroughbred from a small stable. But Hanford, a former rider himself, went to work on Melvyn (Bones) LeBoyne, agent for champion jockey, Eddie Arcaro. "Kelso's a great horse and he's going places," Hanford told Bones. But Bones wouldn't buy it.

"Bones was always like that," Arcaro, now retired and head of a successful livestock insurance firm, told me recently. "But my mount for the Jerome Handicap at Aqueduct was injured just before the race, and Bones let me throw my leg over Kelso. I didn't ride him very well and Kelso won by only a length. 'You just played lucky' Bones told me. 'You don't want to ride him again.' But that was one time I knew better than LeBoyne. I rode Kelso in all his races until I retired at the end of the 1961 season, earned close to $700,000, and won two Horse of the Year awards with him."

"Is that the honor given to the outstanding performance of the year by the Morning Telegraph, the racing man's Bible?" I inquired.

Arcaro nodded. "I've ridden in over 25,000 races," he went on, his expressive face alive with reminiscence, "and I've never ridden a better horse than Kelso."

"What makes Kelso great?" I asked.

Arcaro answered slowly after a moment's thought. "He's great because he wants to run and he wants to win. He's smart enough to cover up for your mistakes, and he'll always give you the final effort."

In 1961 Kelso earned $425,564 and was again named Horse of the Year and in 1962, with his new jockey, Ismael (Milo)

Valenzuela aboard, Kelso joined the exclusive "Millionaire's Club." Now he could hang up his bridle with Citation, Nashua, and Carry Back.

Valenzuela still talks about how his arms were paralyzed for four days after trying to haul Kelso in from his ten-length victory in that year's Jockey Club Gold Cup. The fiery Mexican sheepherder turned jockey is so fond of his caviar and champagne meal ticket, however, that he presented Kelso with a gray and yellow cooler (blanket) with "To Kelso from Milo" emblazoned on both sides.

The Horse of the Year award was his again in 1963 and 1964. Never before had such victories, honors, and citations come to any horse for five successive seasons. But as his bankroll and public swelled to record heights Kelso remained undisturbed. You might think he lives on rare grains and grasses, but actually oats, hay, and Nutragen, a vitamin supplement, are his only foods. He drinks Mountain Valley bottled water at $1.00 a gallon and likes to sleep on Stazdry, the trade name for chopped sugar cane.

His following is so tremendous that before race time thousands flock to see him. So that the champ can get his rest an equine stand-in does the honors. While Kelso remains hidden from view his fans happily lavish sugar and admiration on a substitute brown gelding, Kelly's double. But he can't get away from the crowds in the paddock. Like Joe Louis in the old days making his way to the ring for a championship bout, Kelso needs uniformed Pinkertons to clear his path to the track.

Fourteen-year-old Heather Noble of Virginia started his fan club. She saw Kelso for the first time on TV in 1960. "That horse is looking at me," she told her mother. "What's his name?" Soon she was cheering him at the track, waving Kelso banners and always wearing gray and yellow, Kelso's colors, when he ran. The club's membership of well over a thousand girls adore their hero and at race time they all wear yellow ribbons in their hair.

He often jets to his appointments, but as is the case with so many veteran flyers dropping from the sky for a landing makes him nervous. As soon as the plane starts to descend he likes to have people around, and if left alone he becomes restless and nickers.

More than 50 letters a day and sacks of Christmas cards find their way to Kelso's personal mail box at Woodstock Farm. Lumps of sugar, slightly granulated in transit, arrive frequently, and visitors bring bushels of carrots. Kelso in turn hands out ash trays with his picture on them.

Kelly is not home often, but when he is life is full of privileges. If the weather is bad, he has to do his calisthenics on the indoor track; if it is good, he hacks cross-country with his mistress. With Dick Jenkins, his exercise boy, in the saddle, the champ follows Mrs. duPont over the Maryland countryside. The horse who burns up the track at Aqueduct likes to ford streams, stare at cows, and hop over an occasional log when no one is looking.

He lives in Box 1 of Woodstock Farm's impressive gray and yellow race horse barn. Four American flags, commemorating the times he has represented his country in the Washington International, cover his door. Underneath the red, white, and blue a large brass plaque chronicles his amazing record.

Dogs are his playmates and Charlie, a four-legged, mongrel stable bum, shares his stall. Kelly is gentle with him and takes good care never to hurt his canine friend, but the champ is not so kind to elderly "Fitz," his groom. He gets terribly bored with newspaper interviewers and impatient with photographers and has been known to kick over painter's easels. He may nip you a little in search of sugar or strike you with his left foreleg, but generally he means well.

"Racing is his life," Carl Hanford told me, but as the 1964 season rolled around it was pretty well agreed that Kelso could not do it again. He was seven years old, three years older than most of his competition. And the way he started in California bore out the prophets of gloom. In the first two races he failed to place, and in one he never got going and was beaten by 15 lengths.

"Don't push the panic button yet," Carl Hanford advised. Many did. When Kelso reached the New York tracks that season he was beaten twice, and the Brooklyn Handicap almost proved his undoing. He reared as he entered the starting gate, banging his head so hard on the barrier that he was on his knees when the bell rang. Valenzuela pulled him together, but too much time had been lost and they trailed the field.

After that accident which left a bump on his head that is still noticeable today, Hanford let Kelso rest until August. It must have done his horse mind good. In the Mechanicsville Purse at Saratoga he once more showed he was a champion. He equalled the American record for the mile-and-a-sixteenth on turf.

This performance brought him to the $100,000 Aqueduct Stakes at New York's largest track on Labor Day. Kelso was in top form again, but only his fans believed it. The betting public did not. They sent him off at 2-1, his longest odds in 19 months. The odds on Gun Bow were 1-2. The favorite, a four-year old, shot out of the gate first and soon was leading by five lengths. But for the first time all year Kelso was running as though he enjoyed it. His flat powerful strides that he inherited from his great granddaddy Man O'War covered the ground. Kelso put his big heart into it and foot by foot, Gun Bow's lead began to shrink. Suddenly the cheering started. Thousands of spectators roared their encouragement. Relentlessly, Kelso kept coming. At the top of the stretch he was alongside, and when he crossed the finish line, he was 3 lengths in front of Gun Bow. Hard-boiled New Yorkers who lost cold cash by the upset did not stop cheering Kelso for 15 minutes. They tore up their worthless Gun Bow mutuel tickets and hugged each other. To see the old man victorious was worth more than money.

You can't win 'em all! Three weeks later Kelso lost the Woodward Stakes by a hair. But winning the Jockey Club Gold Cup made him the only horse in more than 200 years of American racing to take the cup five times. The great Nashua managed to win it twice, the second time setting a world record of 3:20 2/5 seconds for the two miles. But Kelso has beaten that twice and he now holds the American record for two miles at 3:19 1/5.

The great International Race at Laurel Track near Washington still eluded him. He had placed three times in it previously, but he had never won the classic in which the world's best compete. At two miles Kelso has never been beaten, but the International is a mile-and-a-half and again Gun Bow was the favorite. Horses from England, Ireland, Japan, and the U.S.S.R. didn't stand a chance; only Gun Bow rated. Kelso bided his time, let the youngster take the lead, and then in a driving finish thundered past him, beating his arch rival by four-and-a-half lengths. Walter Blum, Gun Bow's jockey, told reporters with a sigh, "Kelso is just too good for us." Kelly did the mile-and-a-half in two minutes, 23 4/5 seconds, topping both the track record and the American record on grass. And just to make it perfect, winning this race pyramided his earnings to $1,893,362, making him the biggest money winner of all time.

"We'll race him as long as he can beat the best," Carl Hanford has always insisted. And as the 1965 season got underway Kelso continued to demonstrate his superiority over six crops of yearlings—a total of 70,000 horses.

Now that he is eight years old, it takes longer to get Kelso fit, and he hits his peak later in the season, but winning the Whitney in August of last year was about the finest performance of his career. Perhaps one of the reasons for this was the presence of the Right Reverend Arthur McKinstry, retired Episcopal Bishop of Delaware, often referred to as Kelso's private chaplain. He is an old friend of Mrs. duPont and rarely misses a race. When asked if he directed prayers to God on behalf of the race horse, he answered, "I don't have to. Let's say I just sit there with my fingers crossed and hope a little."

The Bishop may not have prayed hard enough during the running of the Stymie Handicap. Kelso won with ease, but during the race a clod of dirt hit him in the eye causing an infection. It did not seem like much, but every time he had a hard workout after that the eye swelled up again.

On the day of the $100,000 Woodward Stakes, Kelso's regular stop toward his now annual Horse of the Year award, trainer Carl Hanford had to scratch him. The veteran horseman took his disappointment stoically, but the crowd of more than 50,000 did not. "I came to see Kelso run, but I won't see anything now," said a man from the Bronx.

"I wouldn't have driven all this distance if I'd known about it sooner," insisted a man from Massachusetts.

"What an anticlimax!" grumbled a third.

Mud in his eye ended the season for the great Kelso. The meet at Aqueduct that should easily have seen him over the $2,000,000 mark and perhaps Horse of the Year again for the sixth unprecedented time left the brown gelding fretting in his stall, rubbing his sore eye, and feeling sorry for himself.

"We still have $22,000 worth of unfinished business," Carl Hanford admits, "but we'll make it. Kelso's like fine old wine, he gets better with age." He looks fondly at his pet. "There'll never be another one like him."

Win or lose, the fans acknowledge Kelso to be the greatest. For seven straight years he has triumphed at every distance—on grass, dirt, mud, and in slop six inches deep.

What he does from here on in matters little. Kelso has left his indelible mark on U.S. racing. He has accomplished far more than breaking countless track and money records. He has instilled the quality of wonder into the hard-bitten, tough-talking, dollar-hungry, racing fraternity. He has given them something to love and admire as well as something to bet on.

# FOXHUNTING

# Modern American Foxhunting

*I am very fond of the selections I have chosen for this section of the book, but I realize that they are about times gone by and have little resemblance to present-day U.S. fox hunting.*

*At this writing, organized fox hunting in the United States consists of one hundred and twelve hunts registered with the Masters of Fox Hounds Association, plus thirty or more unrecognized packs, a substantial increase over twenty-five years ago.*

*Although it may seem unbelievable, several times a week, in fall and winter, two or three thousand men, women, and children from Massachusetts to California mount their horses, listen for the shrill note of the huntsman's horn, and gallop, wide open, over the wintry countryside to follow the hounds who follow the fox.*

*These hunts vary in the number of hounds they keep, the elaborateness of their kennels and stables, the amount of territory they hunt over, and the number of members who help to support the hunt.*

*Mr. Stewart's Cheshire Fox Hounds, a private pack and not a club, is recognized by many to be the outstanding hunt in this country. To give you a feel of what modern hunting is all about,*

*I am including an excerpt from an article about the Cheshire that appeared in 1953, in the original dummy of one of today's outstanding national sporting magazines.*

Twang! twang! twang! goes the horn and jogging down through Little Pinkerton comes the pack—Mr. Stewart's Cheshire Foxhounds—and Mrs. Hannum and the whippers-in. It's cub-hunting time, those few precious fall months before the formal opening of the fox-hunting season, when the huntsman takes his new entry hounds into covert and works them into the pack.

Out by McConnell Farm in the early sunlight the field stands waiting, anxious for the day's sport to begin.

"Here they come," someone cries and 30 couples of massive black and white and tan beauties flock into the meeting place, sterns feathering with eagerness and impatience.

"Morning, Mrs. Hannum," calls out a groom and the velvet-capped Master of Foxhounds, Mrs. John B. Hannum, raises her whip in salute and smiles a greeting to all present. It lacks two minutes of 8 a.m. as she takes a center position, hounds at her feet and stern-faced professional whippers-in at her side. About her horse the hounds walk or sit, the young ones busy with their noses, not having yet learned to husband their strength.

Tooooo-oot! There goes the copper horn announcing time to move out.

Crack, Crack Hi-eee . . . Hieee. . . . The whippers-in round up the hounds and again the huntsman's horn is blown. Slowly the cavalcade moves off to covert. First the huntsman and hounds with whippers-in posted at either side and then the field.

Across the road, through a gate and there stretched out before them is the Brandywine country, ablaze in its multi-colored fall foliage, mysterious now in its early morning shroud of mist. This is the Cheshire's hunting country; gentle valleys carpeted with hazel and oak copse, mile after mile of undulating, open galloping farmland, a covert-filled fox-hunters' paradise set deep into the heart of Chester County, Pa.

Crack! crack! goes the whip again and a too boisterous hound rejoins the pack swinging its way to covert. From her horse Nancy Hannum watches the young hounds all the way. This is their day. For a year now they have been trained for this moment. The way they show themselves now will decide whether they will be "entered" members of the famous pack.

Built and bred into each of these barrel-chested aristocrats loping their way to the hunt is the nose of a bloodhound, the speed of a greyhound and as blood-curdling a cry as can be heard today.

Mr. Stewart's Cheshire Hounds are a huntsman's joy. Once they hit the line they are fury let loose, a spine-chilling, merciless pack of hunters outdistancing horse and field, checking, working, hitting it off again through five hours of relentless chase. Now is the apprentice hounds' big chance to win entry into the working pack. Now the huntsman will make the decision: is Dixie a babbler, noisy and giving tongue too freely? which young'un will make the best cast? who will challenge first and are there flighty ones and skirters among us?

Up past the Jones Farm and on to Trimble's Hollow the procession hacks to covert, the field following on behind. The riders, in twos and fours, rat-catcher dressed, dropping back, now coming forward again, rising in the saddle to the trot-toe--trot, trot-toe-trot, of their thoroughbred horses.

Not all idle rich people of leisure, but farmhands and steelworkers too, rich only in their love of the sport. The Cheshire isn't a flossy hunt, nor a social event with an easy ride and an early home. This is a huntsman's meet, packed with heart-pounding jumps at breakneck speed and a grueling pace which never seems to let up. This is the Noble Science brought to its peak in America, a matchless pack of hounds, handled and led by one of the best masters in the country.

Now they are at covert. They've approached upwind so as not

to give warning to the young fox cub they hunt. In cubbing only the young fox is hunted as the inexperienced hounds would never be able to match their wits against an old and wily fox, who would run rings round them in a minute.

Outside the wood the field stands halted, waiting for hounds to draw. "Eloo-in, Eloo-in . . ." cries Mrs. Hannum, casting hounds into covert with a cheer. The old-timers crash into the undergrowth, noses to the ground. Fanning out, they work every inch of the ground, weaving, doubling back, moving on, their sterns feathering, silently nosing their fox. The young hounds bound in after them, not yet sure why, but not wanting to lose the main pack.

"Yoi . . . rouse him, wind him," calls Mrs. Hannum, her crying, "try-on-on-onnn!" echoing through the still woods as she urges them to draw. Woods and brush come alive with the rustle of dry leaves and breaking bramble as hounds go to work. Then suddenly, an urgent high-pitched yipping sound from good old Raider on the left.

"Speak to it, Raider, Speak to it, good boy." A young hound joins him, nose to the ground, drawing in a scent which sets every hackle on its body stiff with delight, and together young and old throw up their heads and send out music from their hearts.

"Hark to Raider, Hark to Raider . . . Whoooo-op, Whoooo-op," cries Nancy Hannum, digging in her spurs and bolting after the black and tan blur ahead of her. And then every hound is on it and a chorus of roaring and loud ringing mouths shatters the crystal air as hounds are "Gone Away."

The field takes after them over hedge and rail, disappearing into the distance, hanging on to their charging steeds for dear life, with a prayer at their lips at every fence.

Later in the afternoon they return, the huntsman, the hounds and what is left of the field. The hounds, some limping, bramble-scratched and lame are exhausted, filthy but triumphant. Like the novice rider in the field they have been blooded to their first fox. They've made mistakes, been whipped at, scolded and praised, but in their nose still rankles a scent they will never forget.

With dusk settling over the Brandywine a mud-spattered and tired Mrs. Hannum jogs them back to the kennels, knowing now for sure that the coming season will have a pack as good as ever.

# How the Brigadier Slew the Fox

*from* THE ADVENTURES OF GERARD

*by Sir Arthur Conan Doyle*

*Most of us have read Sir Arthur Conan Doyle's exciting Sherlock Holmes mysteries, but few have come across this little-known tale of the Napoleonic wars. In "How the Brigadier Slew the Fox" Doyle writes of a nineteenth-century war equal in importance to the two great conflicts of the twentieth century. It changed the map of Europe and thousands were killed, but it was a gentleman's war. In the Duke of Wellington's day British officers, including their commander-in-chief, found time for their favorite sport—fox hunting. With their imported English hounds streaming in front of them, they would gallop over the Portuguese countryside, worrying little about the enemy often encamped only a few miles away.*

*In this story Conan Doyle gives us a sporting sidelight into the Peninsular Campaign, as well as a delightful spoof at the English and their habit of taking fox hunting too seriously.*

In all the great hosts of France there was only one officer toward whom the English of Wellington's Army retained a deep, steady, and unchangeable hatred. There were plunderers among the French, and men of violence, gamblers, duellists, and *roués*. All these could be forgiven, for others of their kidney were to be found among the ranks of the English. But one officer of Massena's force had committed a crime which was unspeakable, unheard of, abominable; only to be alluded to with curses late in the evening, when a second bottle had loosened the tongues of men. The news of it was carried back to England, and country gentlemen who knew little of the details of the war grew crimson with passion when they heard of it, and yeomen of the shires raised freckled fists to Heaven and swore. And yet who should be the doer of this dreadful deed but our friend the Brigadier, Etienne Gerard, of the Hussars of Conflans, gay-riding, plume-tossing, debonair, the darling of the ladies and of the six brigades of light cavalry.

But the strange part of it is that this gallant gentleman did this hateful thing, and made himself the most unpopular man in the Peninsula, without ever knowing that he had done a crime for which there is hardly a name amid all the resources of our language. He died of old age, and never once in that imperturbable self-confidence which adorned or disfigured his character knew that so many thousand Englishmen would gladly have hanged him with their own hands. On the contrary, he numbered this adventure among those other exploits which he has given to the world, and many a time he chuckled and hugged himself as he narrated it to the eager circle who gathered round him in that humble café where, between his dinner and his dominoes, he would tell, amid tears and laughter, of that inconceivable Napoleonic past when France, like an angel of wrath, rose up, splendid and terrible, before a cowering continent. Let us listen to him as he tells the story in his own way and from his own point of view.

You must know, my friends, said he, that it was toward the end of the year eighteen hundred and ten that I and Massena and the others pushed Wellington backward until we had hoped to drive him and his army into the Tagus. But when we were still twenty-five miles from Lisbon we found that we were betrayed, for what had this Englishman done but build an enormous line of works and forts at a place called Torres Vedras, so that even we were unable to get through them! They lay across the whole Peninsula, and our army was so far from home that we did not dare to risk a reverse, and we had already learned at Busaco that it was no child's play to fight against these people. What could we do, then, but sit down in front of these lines and blockade them to the best of our power? There we remained for six months, amid such anxieties that Massena said afterward that he had not one hair which was not white upon his body. For my own part, I did not worry much about our situation, but I looked after our horses, who were in much need of rest and green fodder. For the rest, we drank the wine of the country and passed the time as best we might. There was a lady at Santarem—but my lips are sealed. It is the part of a gallant man to say nothing, though he may indicate that he could say a great deal.

One day Massena sent for me, and I found him in his tent with a great plan pinned upon the table. He looked at me in silence with that single piercing eye of his, and I felt by his expression that the matter was serious. He was nervous and ill at ease, but my bearing seemed to reassure him. It is good to be in contact with brave men.

"Colonel Etienne Gerard," said he, "I have always heard that you are a very gallant and enterprising officer."

It was not for me to confirm such a report, and yet it would be folly to deny it, so I clinked my spurs together and saluted.

"You are also an excellent rider."

I admitted it.

"And the best swordsman in the six brigades of light cavalry."

Massena was famous for the accuracy of his information.

"Now," said he, "if you will look at this plan you will have no difficulty in understanding what it is that I wish you to do. These are the lines of Torres Vedras. Yon will perceive that they cover a vast space, and you will realise that the English can only hold a position here and there. Once through the lines you have twenty-five miles of open country which lie between them and Lisbon. It is very important to me to learn how Wellington's troops are distributed throughout that space, and it is my wish that you should go and ascertain."

His words turned me cold.

"Sir," said I, "it is impossible that a colonel of light cavalry should condescend to act as a spy."

He laughed and clapped me on the shoulder.

"You would not be a Hussar if you were not a hot-head," said he. "If you will listen you will understand that I have not asked you to act as a spy. What do you think of that horse?"

He had conducted me to the opening of his tent, and there was a *chasseur* who led up and down a most admirable creature. He was a dapple grey, not very tall, a little over fifteen hands perhaps, but with the short head and splendid arch of the neck which comes with the Arab blood. His shoulders and haunches were so muscular, and yet his legs so fine, that it thrilled me with joy just to gaze upon him. A fine horse or a beautiful woman—I cannot look at them unmoved, even now when seventy winters have chilled my blood. You can think how it was in the year '10.

"This," said Massena, "is Voltigeur, the swiftest horse in our army. What I desire is that you should start tonight, ride round the lines upon the flank, make your way across the enemy's rear, and return upon the other flank, bringing me news of his disposition. You will wear a uniform, and will, therefore, if captured, be safe from the death of a spy. It is probable that you will get through the lines unchallenged, for the posts are very scattered. Once through, in daylight you can outride anything which you meet, and if you keep off the roads you may escape entirely unnoticed. If you have not reported yourself by tomorrow night, I will understand that you are taken, and I will offer them Colonel Petrie in exchange."

Ah, how my heart swelled with pride and joy as I sprang into the saddle and galloped this grand horse up and down to show the Marshal the mastery which I had of him! He was magnificent —we were both magnificent, for Massena clapped his hands and cried out in his delight. It was not I, but he, who said that a gallant beast deserves a gallant rider. Then, when for the third time, with my panache flying and my dolman streaming behind me, I thundered past him, I saw upon his hard old face that he had no longer any doubt that he had chosen the man for his purpose. I drew my sabre, raised the hilt to my lips in salute, and galloped on to my own quarters. Already the news had spread that I had been chosen for a mission, and my little rascals came swarming out of their tents to cheer me. Ah! it brings the tears to my old eyes when I think how proud they were of their Colonel. And I was proud of them also. They deserved a dashing leader.

The night promised to be a stormy one, which was very much to my liking. It was my desire to keep my departure most secret, for it was evident that if the English heard that I had been detached from the army they would naturally conclude that something important was about to happen. My horse was taken, therefore, beyond the picket line, as if for watering, and I followed and mounted him there. I had a map, a compass, and a paper of instructions from the Marshal, and with these in the bosom of my tunic and my sabre at my side I set out upon my adventure.

A thin rain was falling and there was no moon, so you may imagine that it was not very cheerful. But my heart was light at the thought of the honour which had been done me and the glory which awaited me. This exploit should be one more in that brilliant series which was to change my sabre into a *bâton*. Ah, how we dreamed, we foolish fellows, young, and drunk with success! Could I have foreseen that night as I rode, the chosen man of sixty thousand, that I should spend my life planting cabbages on a hundred francs a month! Oh, my youth, my hopes, my comrades! But the wheel turns and never stops. Forgive me, my friends, for an old man has his weakness.

My route, then, lay across the face of the high ground of Torres Vedras, then over a streamlet, past a farmhouse which had been burned down and was now only a landmark, then through a forest of young cork oaks, and so to the monastery of San Antonio, which marked the left of the English position. Here I turned south and rode quietly over the downs, for it was at this point that Massena thought that it would be most easy for me to find my way unobserved through the position. I went very slowly, for it was so dark that I could not see my hand in front of me. In such cases I leave my bridle loose and let my horse pick its own way. Voltigeur went confidently forward, and I was very content to sit upon his back and to peer about me, avoiding every light. For three hours we advanced in this cautious way, until it seemed to me that I must have left all danger behind me. I then pushed on more briskly, for I wished to be in the rear of the whole army by daybreak. There are many vineyards in these parts which in winter become open plains, and a horseman finds new difficulties in his way.

But Massena had underrated the cunning of these English, for it appears that there was not one line of defence but three, and it was the third, which was the most formidable, through which I was at that instant passing. As I rode, elated at my own success, a lantern flashed suddenly before me, and I saw the glint of polished gun-barrels and the gleam of a red coat.

"Who goes there?" cried a voice—such a voice! I swerved to the right and rode like a madman, but a dozen squirts of fire came out of the darkness, and the bullets whizzed all round my ears. That was no new sound to me, my friends, though I will not talk like a foolish conscript and say that I have ever liked it. But at least it had never kept me from thinking clearly, and so I knew that there was nothing for it but to gallop hard and try my luck elsewhere. I rode round the English picket, and then, as I heard nothing more of them, I concluded rightly that I had at last come through their defences. For five miles I rode south, striking a tinder from time to time to look at my pocket compass. And then in an instant—I feel the pang once more as my memory brings back the moment—my horse, without a sob or stagger, fell stone-dead beneath me!

I had never known it, but one of the bullets from that infernal picket had passed through his body. The gallant creature had never winced nor weakned, but had gone while life was in him. One instant I was secure on the swiftest, most graceful horse in Massena's army. The next he lay upon his side, worth only the price of his hide, and I stood there that most helpless, most ungainly of creatures, a dismounted Hussar. What could I do with my boots, my spurs, my trailing sabre? I was far inside the enemy's lines. How could I hope to get back again? I am not ashamed to say that I, Etienne Gerard, sat upon my dead horse and sank my face in my hands in my despair. Already the first streaks were whitening the east. In half an hour it would be light. That I should have won my way past every obstacle and then at this last instant be left at the mercy of my enemies, my mission ruined, and myself a prisoner—was it not enough to break a soldier's heart?

But courage, my friends! We have these moments of weakness, the bravest of us; but I have a spirit like a slip of steel, for the more you bend it the higher it springs. One spasm of despair, and then a brain of ice and a heart of fire. All was not yet lost. I who had come through so many hazards would come through this one also. I rose from my horse and considered what had best be done.

And first of all it was certain that I could not get back. Long before I could pass the lines it would be broad daylight. I must hide myself for the day, and then devote the next night to my escape. I took the saddle, holsters, and bridle from poor Voltigeur, and I concealed them among some bushes, so that no one finding him could know that he was a French horse. Then, leaving him lying there, I wandered on in search of some place where I might be safe for the day. In every direction I could see camp fires upon the sides of the hills, and already figures had begun to move around them. I must hide quickly, or I was lost.

But where was I to hide? It was a vineyard in which I found myself, the poles of the vines still standing, but the plants gone. There was no cover. Besides, I should want some wood and water before another night had come. I hurried wildly onward through the waning darkness, trusting that chance would be my friend. And I was not disappointed. Chance is a woman, my friends, and she has her eye always upon a gallant Hussar.

Well, then, as I stumbled through the vineyard, something loomed in front of me, and I came upon a great square house with another long, low building upon one side of it. Three roads met there, and it was easy to see that this was the posada, or wine-shop. There was no light in the windows, and everything was dark and silent, but, of course, I knew that such comfortable quarters were certainly occupied, and probably by someone of importance. I have learned, however, that the nearer the danger may really be the safer place, and so I was by no means inclined to trust myself away from this shelter. The low building was evidently the stable, and into this I crept, for the door was unlatched. The place was full of bullocks and sheep, gathered there, no doubt, to be out of the clutches of marauders. A ladder led to a loft, and up this I climbed and concealed myself very snugly among some bales of hay upon the top. This loft had a small open window, and I was able to look down upon the front of the inn and also upon the road. There I crouched and waited to see what would happen.

It was soon evident that I had not been mistaken when I had thought that this might be the quarters of some person of importance. Shortly after daybreak an English light dragoon arrived with a despatch, and from then onward the place was in a turmoil, officers continually riding up and away. Always the same name was upon their lips: "Sir Stapleton—Sir Stapleton." It was hard for me to lie there with a dry moustache and watch the great flagons which were brought out by the landlord to these English officers. But it amused me to look at their fresh-coloured, clean-shaven, careless faces, and to wonder what they would think if they knew that so celebrated a person was lying so near to them. And then, as I lay and watched, I saw a sight which filled me with surprise.

It is incredible the insolence of these English! What do you suppose Milord Wellington had done when he found that Massena had blockaded him and that he could not move his army? I might give you many guesses. You might say that he had raged, that he had despaired, that he had brought his troops together and spoken to them about glory and the fatherland before leading them to one last battle. No, Milord did none of these things. But he sent a fleet ship to England to bring him a number of fox-dogs, and he with his officers settled himself down to chase the fox. It is true what I tell you. Behind the lines of Torres Vedras these mad Englishmen made the fox chase three days in the week. We had heard of it in the camp, and now I was myself to see that it was true.

For, along the road which I have described, there came these very dogs, thirty or forty of them, white and brown, each with its tail at the same angle, like the bayonets of the Old Guard. My faith, but it was a pretty sight! And behind and amidst them there rode three men with peaked caps and red coats, whom I understood to be the hunters. After them came many horsemen with uniforms of various kinds, stringing along the roads in twos and threes, talking together and laughing. They did not seem to be going above a trot, and it appeared to me that it must indeed be a slow fox which they hoped to catch. However, it was their affair, not mine, and soon they had all passed my window and were out of sight. I waited and I watched, ready for any chance which might offer.

Presently an officer, in a blue uniform not unlike that of our flying artillery, came cantering down the road—an elderly, stout man he was, with grey side-whiskers. He stopped and began to talk with an orderly officer of dragoons, who waited outside the inn, and it was then that I learned the advantage of the English which had been taught me. I could hear and understand all that was said.

"Where is the meet?" said the officer, and I thought that he was hungering for his bifstek. But the other answered him that it was near Altara, so I saw that it was a place of which he spoke.

"You are late, Sir George," said the orderly.

"Yes, I had a court-martial. Has Sir Stapleton Cotton gone?"

At this moment a window opened, and a handsome young man in a very splendid uniform looked out of it.

"Halloa, Murray!" said he. "These cursed papers keep me, but I will be at your heels."

"Very good, Cotton. I am late already, so I will ride on."

"You might order my groom to bring round my horse," said the young General at the window to the orderly below, while the other went on down the road.

The orderly rode away to some outlying stable, and then in a few minutes there came a smart English groom with a cockade in his hat, leading by the bridle a horse—and, oh, my friends, you have never known the perfection to which a horse can attain until you have seen a first-class English hunter. He was superb: tall, broad, strong, and yet as graceful and agile as a deer. Coal black he was in colour, and his neck, and his shoulder, and his quarters, and his fetlocks—how can I describe him all to you? The sun shone upon him as on polished ebony, and he raised his hoofs in a little playful dance so lightly and prettily, while he tossed his mane and whinnied with impatience. Never have I seen such a mixture of strength and beauty and grace. I had often wondered how the English Hussars had managed to ride over the *chasseurs* of the Guards in the affair at Astorga, but I wondered no longer when I saw the English horses.

There was a ring for fastening bridles at the door of the inn, and the groom tied the horse there while he entered the house. In an instant I had seen the chance which Fate had brought to me. Were I in that saddle I should be better off than when I started. Even Voltigeur could not compare with this magnificent creature. To think is to act with me. In one instant I was down the ladder and at the door of the stable. The next I was out and the bridle was in my hand. I bounded into the saddle. Somebody, the master or the man, shouted wildly behind me. What cared I for his shouts! I touched the horse with my spurs and he bounced forward with such a spring that only a rider like myself could have sat him. I gave him his head and let him go—it did not matter to me where, so long as we left this inn far behind us. He thundered away across the vineyards, and in a very few minutes I had placed miles between myself and my pursuers. They could no longer tell in that wild country in which direction I had gone. I knew that I was safe, and so, riding to the top of a small hill, I drew my pencil and note-book from my pocket and proceeded to make plans of those camps which I could see and to draw the outline of the country.

He was a dear creature upon whom I sat, but it was not easy to draw upon his back, for every now and then his two ears would cock, and he would start and quiver with impatience. At first I could not understand this trick of his, but soon I observed that he only did it when a peculiar noise—"yoy, yoy, yoy"—came from somewhere among the oak woods beneath us. And then suddenly this strange cry changed into a most terrible screaming, with the frantic blowing of a horn. Instantly he went mad—this horse. His eyes blazed. His mane bristled. He bounded from the earth and bounded again, twisting and turning in a frenzy. My pencil flew one way and my note-book another. And then, as I looked down into the valley, an extraordinary sight met my eyes. The hunt was streaming down it. The fox I could not see, but the dogs were in full cry, their noses down, their tails up, so close together that they might have been one great yellow and white moving carpet. And behind them rode the horsemen—my faith, what a sight! Consider every type which a great army could show. Some in hunting dress, but the most in uniforms: blue dragoons, red dragoons, red-trousered hussars, green riflemen, artillerymen, gold-slashed lancers, and most of all red, red, red for the infantry officers ride as hard as the cavalry. Such a crowd, some well mounted, some ill, but all flying along as best they might, the subaltern as good as the general, jostling and pushing, spurring and driving, with every thought thrown to the winds save that they should have the blood of this absurd fox! Truly, they are an extraordinary people, the English!

But I had little time to watch the hunt or to marvel at these islanders, for of all these mad creatures the very horse upon which I sat was the maddest. You understand that he was himself a hunter, and that the crying of these dogs was to him what the call of a cavalry trumpet in the street yonder would be to me. It thrilled him. It drove him wild. Again and again he bounded into the air, and then, seizing the bit between his teeth, he plunged down the slope and galloped after the dogs. I swore, and tugged, and pulled, but I was powerless. This English General rode his horse with a snaffle only, and the beast had a mouth of iron. It was useless to pull him back. One might as well try to keep a grenadier from a wine-bottle. I gave it up in despair, and, settling down in the saddle, I prepared for the worst which could befall.

What a creature he was! Never have I felt such a horse between my knees. His great haunches gathered under him with every stride, and he shot forward ever faster and faster, stretched like a greyhound, while the wind beat in my face and whistled past my ears. I was wearing our undress jacket, a uniform simple and dark in itself—though some figures give distinction to any uniform—and I had taken the precaution to remove the long panache from my busby. The result was that, amidst the mixture of costumes in the hunt, there was no reason why mine should attract attention, or why these men, whose thoughts were all with the chase, should give any heed to me. The idea that a French officer might be riding with them was too absurd to enter their minds. I laughed as I rode, for, indeed, amid all the danger, there was something of comic in the situation.

I have said that the hunters were very unequally mounted, and so at the end of a few miles, instead of being one body of men, like a charging regiment, they were scattered over a considerable space, the better riders well up to the dogs and the others trailing away behind. Now, I was as good a rider as any, and my horse was the best of them all, and so you can imagine that it was not long before he carried me to the front. And when I saw the dogs streaming over the open, and the red-coated huntsman behind them, and only seven or eight horsemen between us, then it was that the strangest thing of all happened, for I, too, went mad—I, Etienne Gerard! In a moment it came upon me, this spirit of sport, this desire to excel, this hatred of the fox. Accursed animal, should he then defy us? Vile robber, his hour was come! Ah, it is a great feeling, this feeling of sport, my friends, this desire to trample the fox under the hoofs of your horse. I have made the fox chase with the English. I have also, as I may tell you some day, fought the box-fight with the Bustler, of Bristol. And I say to you that this sport is a wonderful thing—full of interest as well as madness.

The farther we went the faster galloped my horse, and soon there were but three men as near the dogs as I was. All thought of fear of discovery had vanished. My brain throbbed, my blood ran hot—only one thing upon earth seemed worth living for, and that was to overtake this infernal fox. I passed one of the horsemen—a Hussar like myself. There were only two in front of me now: the one in a black coat, the other the blue artilleryman whom I had seen at the inn. His grey whiskers streamed in the wind, but he rode magnificently. For a mile or more we kept in this order; and then, as we galloped up a steep slope, my lighter weight brought me to the front. I passed them both, and when I reached the crown I was riding level with the little, hard-faced English huntsman. In front of us were the dogs, and then, a hundred paces beyond them, was a brown wisp of a thing, the fox itself, stretched to the uttermost. The sight of him fired my blood. "Aha, we have you then, assassin!" I cried, and shouted my encouragement to the huntsman. I waved my hand to show him that there was one upon whom he could rely.

And now there were only the dogs between me and my prey. These dogs, whose duty it is to point out the game, were now rather a hindrance than a help to us, for it was hard to know how to pass them. The huntsman felt the difficulty as much as I, for he rode behind them, and could make no progress toward the fox. He was a swift rider, but wanting in enterprise. For my part, I felt that it would be unworthy of the Hussars of Conflans if I could not overcome such a difficulty as this. Was Etienne Gerard to be stopped by a herd of fox-dogs? It was absurd. I gave a shout and spurred my horse.

"Hold hard, sir! Hold hard!" cried the huntsman.

He was uneasy for me, this good old man, but I reassured him by a wave and a smile. The dogs opened in front of me. One or two may have been hurt, but what would you have? The egg must be broken for the omelette. I could hear the huntsman shouting his congratulations behind me. One more effort, and the dogs were all behind me. Only the fox was in front.

Ah, the joy and pride of that moment! To know that I had beaten the English at their own sport. Here were three hundred, all thirsting for the life of this animal, and yet it was I who was about to take it. I thought of my comrades of the light cavalry brigade, of my mother, of the Emperor, of France. I had brought honour to each and all. Every instant brought me nearer to the fox. The moment for action has arrived, so I unsheathed my sabre. I waved it in the air, and the brave English all shouted behind me.

Only then did I understand how difficult is this fox chase, for one may cut again and again at the creature and never strike him once. He is small, and turns quickly from a blow. At every cut I heard those shouts of encouragement from behind me, and they spurred me to yet another effort. And then at last the supreme moment of my triumph arrived. In the very act of turning I caught him fair with such another back-handed cut as that with which I killed the aide-de-camp of the Emperor of Russia. He flew into two pieces, his head one way and his tail another. I looked back and waved the blood-stained sabre in the air. For the moment I was exalted—superb!

Ah! how I should have loved to have waited to have received the congratulations of these generous enemies. There were fifty of them in sight, and not one who was not waving his hand and shouting. They are not really such a phlegmatic race, the English. A gallant deed in war or in sport will always warm their hearts. As to the old huntsman, he was the nearest to me, and I could see with my own eyes how overcome he was by what he had seen. He was like a man paralysed, his mouth open, his hand, with outspread fingers, raised in the air. For a moment my inclination was to return and to embrace him.

But already the call of duty was sounding in my ears, and these English, in spite of all the fraternity which exists among sportsmen, would certainly have made me prisoner. There was no hope for my mission now, and I had done all that I could do. I could see the lines of Massena's camp no very great distance off, for, by a lucky chance, the chase had taken us in that direction. I turned from the dead fox, saluted with my sabre, and galloped away.

But they would not leave me so easily, these gallant huntsmen. I was the fox now, and the chase swept bravely over the plain.

It was only at the moment when I started for the camp that they could have known that I was a Frenchman, and now the whole swarm of them were at my heels. We were within gunshot of our pickets before they would halt, and then they stood in knots and would not go away, but shouted and waved their hands at me. No, I will not think that it was in enmity. Rather would I fancy that a glow of admiration filled their breasts, and that their one desire was to embrace the stranger who had carried himself so gallantly and well.

# Peter

*from* THE MILLBECK HOUNDS

*by Gordon Grand*

*"Peter" is one of the lesser known stories of Gordon Grand, considered by many to be the best author of American foxhunting literature.*

*A wealthy lawyer, businessman and country squire, Grand never thought of himself as a professional writer. His first book,* The Silver Horn, *was published in 1932, the year he retired from practicing law, and chronicled the life of a fox hunting community in Dutchess County, New York. He wrote in a gentle, sentimental fashion of a long-gone era where a butler and several maids were a necessity and no sporting gentleman could run a stable without a head groom and several assistants.*

*Colonel Weatherford, the personification of an English country squire, was Gordon Grand's ideal, and plays the central figure in many of his books and short stories. The Colonel's buddy, Mr. Pendleton, Enid Ashley, horsewoman extraordinary, and Eddie Walsh, the entertaining Irish groom, make up the team.*

*Writing about a world he knew so well, Gordon Grand preserves for his readers the charm, joys, sorrows, and feats of sportsmanship of a generation that has all but disappeared in the frenzied whirl of the 1970s.*

*Mr. Grand died in 1950.*

When, towards the end of an early December afternoon, I entered Colonel Weatherford's library, some affair of high moment was taking place in that habitually peaceful, dignified room. Sitting on the extreme edge of one of the Colonel's huge leather armchairs was a very small boy not above nine years of age, his tear-stained, frightened little face and anxious eyes following the Colonel's precipitate movements up and down the room. "This Mr. Redman," the Colonel was saying, "this Mr. Redman of yours, whoever he may be, is—is—is a d—— impudent rascal. Bless my soul, I never heard of such impudence."

At this stage the Colonel looked up and saw me. "Hello Pendleton, hello. Come in, come on. Sit down. Pull up to the fire. This young gentleman," glaring at the boy, "is a most astonishing visitor. There is no reasoning with him. Now then, here's the situation. Some time ago I instructed the kennels to put down that old *Laborer* hound. He has turned babbler. Madden, instead of doing what I told him to do, has had the hound loose around his cottage—like a house dog. This young gentleman, who says that his name is Peter Berrensford, an Irish boy, has been in this country only a month or so and is living over with the Perry Wyndhams. He has fallen in love with old *Laborer,* and the hound with him. The boy wants the hound as his very own, as he puts it, and says he wants him more than he has ever wanted anything in his life, and can't sleep at night or do his lessons or do anything because he thinks Madden may put the hound down at any moment.

"Pendleton, you know how I feel about giving hounds away and having them night-hunting all over the place, disturbing the coverts, pestering the vixens in the spring, taking to killing chickens and getting us into hot water. No one ever keeps them tied up. I like this boy." Upon saying this the Colonel turned and scowled at the poor little distressed boy, then continued. "I would get him a dog. D—— it, I would get a dog for any boy who was hungering for one, a terrier or that kind of a dog; but no, he wants *Laborer*—says that he must have him—that the Hunt mustn't destroy him—says that he and the hound take walks together every afternoon and that the hound came all the way to school today to find him and tell him it was time to go walking and hunting. They are going to hunt rabbits together when Peter can get a gun.

"But Pendleton, that's not all. You haven't heard half of it. That wasn't the part that irritated me. Peter has a friend—some old fellow by the name of Mr. Redman. I never heard of him around here, but the rascal has been putting notions into the boy's head about getting this hound. I suppose he wants him for himself."

The Colonel turned towards the boy. "Now, Peter, let us understand about this Mr. Redman. You say that he is a friend of yours?"

"Yes, sir. He is my best friend. He is the only one I have, except *Laborer*."

"What? The only one, God bless me. Haven't you any friends of your own age—any boys or girls to play with?"

"No, sir. I don't know any one here, only Mr. Redman and Mr. Madden, the huntsman, and—and you, sir—but Mr. Redman is my only friend."

"Well, Peter, you say that Mr. Redman told you to come to see me?"

"Yes, sir. Mr. Redman said that if I came to see Colonel Weatherford, he wouldn't let them kill *Laborer* if he knew that a little boy was fond of the hound and wanted him so terribly much. Mr. Redman said I was not to be frightened or to care what you said or pay any attention to it because everything would be all right."

"There you are, Pendleton, there you are. A man I don't know, never even heard of, tells this little boy that I will give him a hound, that the boy is not to pay any attention to what I say, that—that—well, it's a piece of impertinence."

"Please, sir," continued the boy, "Mr. Redman says that you

don't know him but that he knows you very well and likes you and that some day you are going to hunt with him and Mr. Peter Beckford and Mr. Meynell and Mr. Assheton Smith and Lord Willoughby de Broke. These are friends of Mr. Redman's. Please, sir, Mr. Redman said I was to tell you that he watched you on Thanksgiving Day when you were hunting the hounds yourself and killed away off in the north country. He said, 'Peter, Colonel Weatherford is a fine huntsman. Most huntsmen would have lost their fox that day because they would have dropped too far behind him, when hounds checked in the plow.' Then Mr. Redman told me about it."

The Colonel's massive mouth was partly opened and his deep-set steely eyes were glued to the boy—fairly glaring at him. Had I not known so well that there was no relation between the Colonel's heart and his occasional domineering manner, I could but have resented his frightening so gentle a little boy. The Colonel crossed the room and stood towering above him. "Mr. Redman told you about it. Told you what? What did he tell you?"

"Why, why, Mr. Redman said, 'Peter, Colonel Weatherford's hounds were running in fine cry. They were stooping to it, Peter, and working wonderfully. The pace was getting better and better and the Colonel was creeping right up on his fox, when all at once hounds checked.' That means stopped, sir."

"Yes, yes, boy, I know. Go on. Go on."

"Well, Mr. Redman said you caught hold of your hounds just as soon as they checked, and galloped straight forward with them across the plow, then saw the fox against the sky line on South Millerton Hill, carried hounds on up to the top, clapped them on the fox's back, and they raced for Millerton Uplands. Mr. Redman is teaching me how to hunt hounds, sir, and said that most American huntsmen would have pottered about at that check, but that it was no time to potter about, and if you had pottered you would never have killed your fox. That's what Mr. Redman said, sir."

The Colonel walked over to the table and did what I had not

seen him do in twenty years. He mixed himself a second whiskey and soda, held it in his hand and stood looking into the fire. The room was very quiet. Twice the Colonel turned and studied the boy, then resumed his contemplation of the fire. Suddenly he rose, took an impetuous turn of the room, summoned the chauffeur and instructed him to take Peter home. He was to stop at the kennels en route and tell Will Madden, the huntsman, to put *Laborer* in the car.

Thinking to avail myself of a ride home with Peter, I went out in the hall to gather up my spurs, whip and hat. Peter located his things and we returned to the library to wait the car. The boy's lips were trembling with some deep emotion; relief, I thought, from the dread, haunting picture of the approaching end of old *Laborer,* his friend and companion of the hills. He made a valiant little effort to pull himself together, walked up to the Colonel and said, "Thank you very much, sir, and Mr. Redman, told me I was to promise you that I would take good care of *Laborer,* and I will, sir." The Colonel didn't say anything, but held out his hand, and they shook hands. The boy started to turn away, hesitated, then asked, "Please, sir, was my hound hunting Thanksgiving Day?"

The Colonel went to his desk, picked up the Hunt diary, thumbed the pages, located the Thanksgiving Day run, read through the first part of it hastily to himself, then said, "Here we are: 'Hounds checked at the dusty plow two fields southwest to Millerton Hill. They were well up and pressing their fox, who was making for Three Mile Woods. Wind had freshened to half a blow. I could not afford to potter about, so gathered hounds to me, galloped on with them to deep grass in Benham's Meadow; hounds particularly keen; dropped their heads, spread out like a rocket, hit the line and went on. By good luck I saw the fox on the sky line of Millerton Hill; lifted hounds again and galloped forward to the crest. *Laborer* hit it. Hounds flew to him in spite of his being a notorious babbler—his protest against old age and failing nose. Killed fifteen minutes later at Upper Millington. A game, stout, Thanksgiving Day fox. Seventeen miles from find in Ludlow Woods to kill. Brush to little Mary Sedgwick, mask to Pendleton.' "

From Colonel Weatherford's house to mine is but a step. Sensing that the small boy sitting beside me had many momentous things going on within him, we rode in silence. As the car drew up to my door I turned and wished him good luck with the old hound. He looked up at me and said very solemnly and outspoken, as was his wont, "I'm sorry, sir, that I cried. Mr. Redman won't like that but Colonel Weatherford was terrible cross. Maybe Mr. Redman didn't know how cross he would be."

At dinner my thoughts kept reverting to the small boy with the tense, tear-stained face and pleading eyes. This carried me on to the query of who he was and how he happened to have been brought over to this country from Ireland and be making his home with the Wyndhams, the least suitable of any couple I knew to assume such a responsibility, I did, however, recall that Eunice Wyndham, whom Perry had married in Ireland, was of rarefied lineage, yet of an ungovernable temper and a doubtful past.

A few days later the Colonel's man brought me a note.

"Dear Pendleton:

Read the enclosed. There are times when nothing short of magnificent self-control (not properly appreciated) prevents me from riding roughshod over every law enacted for the preserving of peace and order.

J. W."

I read the letter to which the Colonel referred.

"Col. John Weatherford, M. F. H.,
Millbeck, N. Y.
Dear Colonel Weatherford:

A few days ago my ward, Peter Berrensford, arrived home with a large dog which he states was given to him by you. I was annoyed at this and would be obliged if you would send for the animal at once. I do not permit dogs on my place.

In the last three days Peter has developed even more than ever into a secretive, unresponsive, and over-sentimental young person, a condition I hope to see partially rectified by getting rid of this dreary-eyed dog with which the boy is prone to spend entirely too much time.

Whereas I don't wish to bother you further, yet if you could possibly give me any information respecting a person by the name of Redman I would appreciate such assistance. This individual is exerting a very bad influence on the boy. In spite of repeated punishments Peter stubbornly refuses to divulge any information respecting this man.

Yours truly,
Perry Wyndham"

I returned the letter to its envelope and sent it back by the Colonel's man.

On an afternoon towards the end of the month, the Colonel and I returned from that ever engaging if occasionally exasperating task of training two setter puppies, rapscallions of the first water. Mine had been a fairly satisfactory performance, but the Colonel's seemingly limitless fund of patience had been sorely tried. No man ever contended with a more jubilant, boisterous, devil-may-care, self-willed puppy. The Colonel would plod along hour after hour on such a task, accepting rebuffs, forgiving mockery and really enjoying the battle and never show so much as a tinge of exasperation within hearing of the puppy. He was not, however, always fit company on the ride home.

As we approached his house he finally blurted out, "if you have nothing better to do, Pendleton, come in for a while. I'll have Albert locate a bottle of that Boone's Knoll, Jessamine County, bourbon, Bless me, but that's a sweet title. We will pull up to the fire and have a spot. God, what a puppy!"

Our minds set on this program, we entered the house, to be told that Master Peter Berrensford was waiting in the library to see the Colonel.

The boy was sitting in the same big leather chair. He stood up, twisting his cap around and around in his hands and one look at him told that something was amiss. He seemed frailer than when I had last seen him. Knowing the Colonel's frame of mind I could but have wished that Peter had chosen a more auspicious time for his visit. The Colonel walked briskly up to him. "Now, then, Peter, now then, what is it?" Of all minor signals of distress capable of harassing me, the quivering of a little child's lower lip, spreading to the chin and ending by the biting of the lips in heroic resolve to control emotions, is the most disturbing. Peter started to speak but seemed fearful of releasing his tightly closed lips. Then he suddenly burst forth. "It's the pony. They are going to feed him to the hounds. They are going to do it right away. Mr. Redman said I was——" At that moment a servant entered to tell me that I was wanted on the telephone.

When I returned to the room the Colonel was standing with his back to the fire, with little Peter facing him and looking up at him, still twisting his now misshapen cap. "Well, Pendleton, here is a most extraordinary how-do-you-do. It seems that some one sent an old, one-eyed Shetland pony to the kennels for the hounds. Madden has been letting the pony browse about in the Hunt paddock until he should have use for him. Peter has been going to the kennels every day after school and poking up over the hills on the pony, taking old *Laborer* with him.

"The weather is now turning cold, pasture is scarce and Madden plans to put the pony away and feed him to the hounds. Peter says he is fonder of the pony than of anything else in the world, even *Laborer,* and almost as fond of him as he is of Mr. Redman. Was that what you said, Peter?"

"Yes, sir."

"He says he can't sleep at night, and if he does get to sleep he wakes up frightened for the pony, so he now proposes that the Hunt maintain the pony for him through the winter and until spring grass. God bless me, Pendleton, it's preposterous, preposterous! And where does the boy get such a notion? It's from this Mr. Redman. What was it Mr. Redman told you to do, Peter?"

"Please, sir, he just said I was to come right over and see you quick and tell you about it. He said you would be very cross like you were before and say a lot of God blesses but that I wasn't to mind. And please, sir, I'm not kind of crying, because I'm frightened. I'm not frightened of you any more, sir, but—but—" The boy turned his back to the Colonel, then blurted out, "I—I just keep thinking all the time of my pony—excuse me, sir, your pony—and thinking of what Mr. Madden is going to do. Please, sir, please, please, don't let him do it. Maybe there is some other boy who has a father who could buy him. There must be somebody, sir."

The Colonel walked over to the fireplace, lit his pipe, stood pulling his chin for a moment then said, "Peter, did Mr. Redman tell you anything else to say to me?"

The boy looked embarrassed and hesitant at this question, then answered, "Yes, sir, but please, I don't want to tell it. Perhaps you wouldn't like it, sir."

"Go ahead with it, Peter, go on with it, whatever it was," replied the Colonel.

The boy looked over at me as though needing support, then said, "Well, sir, Mr. Redman told me to tell you that you made a mistake last Tuesday in the way you cast hounds, and that's why you lost the fox. He says that if you are going to use Mr. Thomas Smith's cast you must use all of it and not stop halfway, and not be in a hurry or get impatient just because the field is every place they shouldn't be, and that you must go the whole way round the cast. Mr. Redman says that if you had gone all the way round on

Tuesday you would have hit the line where Mr. Baldwin's woods touch the Stickheap but that you missed that part."

The library had grown quite dark. From where I sat the glow of the firelight was playing on the Colonel's rugged cheek. He stood as one in a trance, yet looking steadily at Peter. The boy was sitting forward, his head resting on his hands. "Peter, do you know what a Thomas Smith cast is?" asked the Colonel.

"No, sir," the boy answered.

"Come over here, Peter, and shake hands with me. The kennels don't belong to me, so I can't keep the pony for you there, and besides there is no empty box, but I'm going to keep him for you at my stable. Eddie Walsh will take care of him and do him well for you. Go over and ring that bell for me."

The Boone's Knoll, Jessamine County, Kentucky, bourbon arrived and with it a piece of cake and a glass of milk for Peter, and we three sat without talking for what must have seemed a long time to a very small boy. Then the Colonel said, "Peter, I gave you a hound. Then when Mr. Wyndham wouldn't let you keep it I brought it back to the kennels and I am keeping it for you. It is still your hound and always will be. I am going to take care of your pony for as long as you want me to. Now don't you think you should tell me who Mr. Redman is? Is his name Redman, Peter?"

The boy thought for a moment, then walked over and stood by the Colonel's chair. "I am sorry, sir, but I can't tell you about Mr. Redman. I will do anything else you want, anything, but Mr. Redman wouldn't want me to tell. He wouldn't like it. I just call him Mr. Redman because he wears a red coat. He is my only friend. If I didn't have him I wouldn't have anybody. Please, sir, don't make me tell. He mightn't come to me again. The only time he didn't come when I wanted him was when I was whipped for being bad. All the other times I was whipped he came right away."

The Colonel drew his hand across his eyes as one who winces

and would erase an unpleasant vision. The car arrived and Peter was sent home, the owner of a pony and in love with the future.

The Colonel and I sat musing upon this frail, odd, appealing little whiff of a neglected boy.

Decades have run their course since the afternoon John Weatherford gave an ancient one-eyed pony to Peter Berrensford to help gladden the boy's short span of life. Those whose paths cross ours occupy places of varying importance in our book of life; some, whole chapters, others but a line. Peter has a short, bright chapter all to himself in my book. Harking back I can still see a small boy on a diminutive, slow-moving, woolly pony, silhouetted against the Millbeck sky line. From some swale an old hound is crying to an ancient line. I have seen them in the early light of morning and in the dusk of autumn days. The Wyndhams were seldom home and the servants let the boy come and go at will, neglected, ill cared for but radiantly happy and contented beyond the lot of most of us.

I would meet them now and again at sunset coming out of the hills, the pony taking his slow deliberate way, old *Laborer* walking at his side. "How are you Peter?" I would ask. "Very well, thank you, Mr. Pendleton. We have been drawing the Stickheap—*Laborer, Nuthatch* and me. It wasn't very good. Please, sir, what does it mean when somebody says the glass is falling? What is the glass? Mr. Redman said the glass was falling and that was why *Laborer* couldn't hunt better."

I explained the situation and he continued, "Mr. Redman was cross today because he thought *Laborer* and I were drawing the McLane covert downwind. We weren't doing that, Mr. Pendleton, but when we were going up the outside of the covert into No Man's Land to draw upwind, *Laborer* smelled something and went right off hunting. He is the wonderfulest smeller, Mr. Pendleton. He was really hunting, but Mr. Redman thought we were drawing. He says that *Laborer* talks so much to his smells and to everything else that it's hard to tell when he is really hunting, but he is a fine hound, Mr. Pendleton."

As we rode along together I asked, "How is *Nuthatch* these days? How is he getting along? He looks very fine—ready for a horse show. Eddie Walsh is doing him well for you."

"Oh, he is top hole and in the pink, thank you, sir. That's what Mr. Redman always says: 'You look top hole and in the pink this morning, Peter my lad.' That's what Mr. Redman says. But I have trouble with him, sir. You see, he is most terribly fond of *Laborer* like I am, because *Laborer* always walks alongside of him when he is not hunting. Then *Laborer* comes over to Colonel Weatherford's every morning to see *Nuthatch* when I am in school. He sleeps in the pony's box all morning. Well, sometimes when we are hunting and *Laborer* gets away way off so we can hardly hear him, *Nuthatch* gets worried or lonesome or something and wants to go and find him. That's what makes all my trouble. You see, sir, I can't stop or steer him when he gets that way. He just goes on and on through the most terrible places. He doesn't trot, just walks, listening and looking for *Laborer*.

"Why, one day last week, sir, he wouldn't turn around till we found *Laborer* away up at Squire Oakleigh's woods. When we got there *Laborer* wouldn't stop hunting for me, but *Nuthatch* started neighing and *Laborer* came to us right away. Dogs smile just like people, don't they, Mr. Pendleton? It was 'most dark when we got home that night, 'cause *Nuthatch* walks so slow. Eddie Walsh says *Laborer* is getting stringhalted in all his legs by holding them up in the air, trying to keep step with *Nuthatch*. That night Mr. Redman laughed and laughed. He said I was the only foxhunter he ever saw, being run away with at a walk. I told Colonel Weatherford about it, and he said he was going to get me a little ship's anchor for Christmas to carry back of the saddle so I could throw it around a tree or a fence post, but I couldn't do that, Mr. Pendleton."

In the pressing activities and interests of each day, one too seldom halts to enjoy the little pleasantries to be found just around the corner. I could have often knocked off for an hour or two and gone a-hunting with Peter and would have been the gainer. He was full of quaint observations and really loved to talk if he felt at home with you. It was as though a flood of thoughts had long been pent up within his little head, most of them connected with Mr. Redman.

He never expounded matters in a way you expected. I came upon him fishing from the footbridge on the kennels road, and stopped to ask him what luck. "Not any, Mr. Pendleton," he answered. "I don't think"—gazing down into the water—"I don't think my worm is trying very hard."

We once passed a freshly despoiled robin's nest. Some of the eggs were yet whole, lying on the ground. Peter stopped the pony. Sorrow and concern crossed his face, and he turned to me, saying, "Mr. Redman once had a little bird in a cage out in India. It was when he was a general there. It laid an egg and sat on it ever so long, but it wouldn't hatch. Then one day Mr. Redman saw the little bird picking up seeds in the cage and trying to feed the seeds to the egg, and he felt very badly and didn't want to kill any of the King's enemies all the rest of that day." It was no wonder that the schoolmistress of the small one-room school at Stevens Corners was forever perplexed at Peter, yet loved him.

I recall how it gave me a mild start to see Peter down in our village. I had never really associated him with stores or people having material needs. He was sitting alone on a big packing case in front of Reardon Briggs' store. "I have a dollar, Mr. Pendleton," he said. "I never had one before. I never had any money before."

"That's fine, Peter. Where did you get it?" He looked up at me with that engaging smile of his, began clicking his heels together and looked down at his swinging feet.

"I don't know whether I should tell you, Mr. Pendleton, but I want to."

"Go ahead, Peter, go ahead," I urged. "I won't tell."

"Well," said Peter, "do you remember the day, last week, when hounds met at the Millbeck School and found a fox in the swamp and ran him right straight for Pugsley Hill? Well, *Laborer, Nuthatch* and I were drawing Mr. Kinney's woods. I tied a string to *Laborer,* and *Nuthatch* and I led him out to the road 'cause we were afraid he would go on with the hounds.

"When I got to the road, Mr. Pettybone Lithgow was coming along. Oh, Mr. Pendleton, he was awfully mad. He was carrying a horseshoe in one hand and said to me, 'Boy, what do you think of a fool horse that casts a shoe at the very start of a run? I feed him all month, then ride him two fields, and he loses me a run. I would knock him on the head for a dollar.'

"Well, Mr. Lithgow rode on down the road and I looked to see what shoe was off, and, Mr. Pendleton, they were all on; so I told Mr. Lithgow. He jumped right off, looked at the shoes, gave me the dollar he was going to get for knocking his horse on the head, jumped up on his horse, gave him what Mr. Redman calls a rib-binder, said he was going to give the man who handed him up the shoe a piece of his mind, and galloped after the hounds. Please, Mr. Pendleton, don't tell anybody because it was nice of Mr. Lithgow to give me a dollar. I never had one before."

Two years later, on a day in mid-May, the thread—a very frail thread, it always seemed to me—which held Peter to us, parted. Our fine old Scotch doctor, Donald McTavish, steeped in experience and wisdom, told me of the end. "Mr. Pendleton, mon, it was better so, better so. I knew the wee laddie well. He could never have been happy grown up. It was never meant to be. He lived with one foot and half of his heart in the sky. Mr. Pendleton, the bairn had a bonnie time. No one in Dutchess County had a better one. People said he was lonesome and solitary and heartsick. You and Kerrnall Wutherford and I know the better."

We sat without speaking for a moment or so, the doctor tapping his foot on the floor. Then he moved his chair closer to me and touched my knee with his finger. This Donald McTavish of ours is a thickset man, with massive shoulders, a grizzled gray beard and a huge sandy-haired head. He is a scholarly man whom Edinburgh has twice honored. "Mr. Pendleton, I stayed with the wee laddie until the end and one thing I ken well; Peter and I were not alone that night. I'm thinking, Mr. Pendleton, that a gentleman—a very great gentleman, and a sportsman—stood by to give the bairn a hand up. About two o'clock Peter whispered to me, 'Doctor, Mr. Redman says I'm not to be afraid. I'm not afraid, Doctor. Mr. Redman told me he would keep hold of my hand all the time. If Mr. Redman said that, then I know he won't let go.' I stepped over to lower the light and when I came back the wee bairn and Mr. Redman had gang awa together."

The old doctor looked down reproachfully at the worn, shabby little bag which had long companioned him in his victories and defeats.

I strolled over to my north window. From this window you can see the south slope of the Stickheap and if you know where to look you can just discern Frahley Hill Lane, winding down from the Stickheap uplands. "*Laborer, Nuthatch* and I drew the Stickheap today, Mr. Pendleton. *Laborer* is the wonderfulest hound, and don't you think *Nuthatch* looks beautiful, Mr. Pendleton? He's most awfully fit.

"Pendleton, mon, come awa, come awa with me to Kerrnal Wutherford's. I gave a promise to the bairn."

We walked slowly across the pleasant, spring-emblazoned meadows separating my farm from the Colonel's. The doctor's tanned, rugged old face seemed doubly lined and furrowed. "Pendleton, the wee burrds are nesting the noo. The fledglings will be along soon. 'Twas nae the time o' the year for us to lose the bairn. Peter,

Ilk hopping bird, wee helpless thing<br>
That in the merry months o' spring

Delighted me to hear thee sing
What comes o' thee?
Where wilt thou cow'r thy chittering wing
And close thy ee?

God tend thee, Peter, lad. God tend thee."

Doctor McTavish handed the Colonel a letter and a flat package done up in brown paper and tied with what looked like a boy's frayed leather shoelace. The Colonel read the letter to himself slowly, word for word, sat quietly for a moment or two; then handed the letter to me.

"Dear Colonel Weatherford:

I am in big trouble. It's about Mr. Redman. I'm afraid they will find him and take him away. You see, sir, I can't get up now. I'm sick. Please, sir, will you help me?

Doctor McTavish is here now. There is no one else here now. I have told the doctor where Mr. Redman is and he is going to take him over to you. Please, sir, be very careful of him. I will come over for him as soon as I can. Mr. Redman told me that if I was ever in big trouble, to tell you. I am in big trouble now. Are the pony and *Laborer* all right?

Mr. Redman comes every night now and stays and stays until I go to sleep, so I am not lonesome. He talks about all the things we are going to do together and says we are going to do them soon. Thank you, sir, for taking care of Mr. Redman.

Peter"

When I looked up, the Colonel was holding the unopened package in his hand. He placed it on the table, and walked over to the window. "Pendleton, the trees are pretty nearly in full leaf upon the Stickheap. In another week we won't be able to see Frahley Hill Road."

"No," I answered, "not in another week."

He walked back to the table, untied the shoelace, opened the package and stood looking at the contents a long time; then handed it to me. It was only a cheap, modern-day, Irish postcard, frayed and wrinkled almost to the point of disintegration; but I looked upon the face of a grave, elderly, sensitive man in velvet cap and scarlet coat. At the bottom of the card was printed: "Peter Charles James Del a Poore Fitzhugh Berrensford, 13th Earl of Cardogan and Baron Kildare, M. F. H. Kildare Hounds 1798–1841. From Portrait by Sir Leslie Spencer, R.A."

# The Tale of Anthony Bell

## *by Sir Alfred Munnings, K.C.V.O.*

*This entertaining poem well deserves to be included in these pages. It is of special interest here because it was written, not by a noted poet, but by the greatest equine artist of the twentieth century.*

*As a painter of horses Sir Alfred had no peer. But he never tried his hand at serious writing until he undertook to pen his autobiography which appeared, a volume a year, from 1950–1953. He did, however, write poems and illustrate them.*

*Sir Alfred, long-time President of the Royal Academy, submitted "The Tale of Anthony Bell" to his friend, John Masefield, Poet Laureate of England. Masefield approved, and it was first published in 1910 in* The Field *Magazine. Later it was included in Munnings' charming book* Ballads and Poems, *printed in 1957.*

The frost is keen, and sparrows unseen
Are fighting amongst the holly;
The hunting is stopped, and the wintry sun
Has tried to thaw where the currents run
In the brook by Steepleton Folly.

It begins to blow, and flakes of snow
Are spitting upon the fire:
  So, sporting children, gather around;
  I'll tell you a story of horse and hound,
And the ways of a hunting squire.

Now, Anthony Bell, of whom I tell,
Was always hunting foxes,
  He lived at a place called Highfield Hall;
  His horses were standing in every stall;
There were horses in all the boxes.

There were browns and bays and wonderful greys,
For greys were his ruling passion;
  And though he had never a guinea to spare,
  He paid three hundred at Horncastle Fair
For a dapple-grey mare called Fashion.

In kennels dry his hounds did lie,
All of them fit for going;
  They found a fox and followed his line,
  Be it ever so wet or ever so fine,
Or the hardest gale were blowing.

His whips and all were hung in the hall;
There were hunting-horns on the tables;
  His boots and trees they stood on the floor,
  And there, on a peg on a green baize door,
Was a coat he wore in the stables.

When his temper boiled he was petted and spoiled
By a wife and three good daughters.
  If he happened to meet with a serious fall,
  They made up a bed in the dining-hall
And sent for old Doctor Waters.

Like a huntsman born, he could wind his horn,
And never a man dare flout him.
  Many were they who did rejoice
  At the sound of his rich, melodious voice
When he rallied his hounds about him.

The Squire's first whip was Daniel Ship,
As keen on a hunt as a spaniel.
  The second whip, Tom, could view a fox
  From Ashton Hill to Clinton Rocks;
He was second to none but Daniel

For miles around good sport they found
On every day but Sunday;
  They hunted as long as the day was light,
  And they all finished up on Saturday night,
And started afresh on Monday.

. . . .

Now, Highfield Hall had chimneys tall:
There were ancient elms about it.
  In one of its rooms a ghost did walk,
  For years it had always been the talk,
And nobody seemed to doubt it.

In Highfield Park, when nights were dark,
The ghost would walk the valley;
  One frosty night, when the moon shone bright,
  The Squire and Daniel followed its flight
The length of the yew-tree alley.

But ghosts of the dead never bothered his head—
A hardened and tough old sinner.
  To keep up his hunting he'd pinch and screw;
  His wife and his daughters they made the stew,
And a groom brought in the dinner.

He returned one day from far away;
His face with the wind was ruddy.
  He'd had such a hunt, his coat was torn;
  He'd lost a spur, he'd lost his horn;
His breeches and boots were muddy.

He called for a drink, and changed his pink
For a seedy old coat worn thinner.
  They brought him his slippers, they brought him
    the jack;
  He pulled off his boots, he was glad to be back,
And then he sat down to dinner.

At half-past nine he had finished his wine;
At ten he began to snore;
  At twelve he was still in his grandfather chair,
  Dreaming he rode on the dapple-grey mare—
When somebody tapped at the door!

. . . . .

By a brandy flask a fox's mask
Was hanging below the ceiling;
  It began to yawn at the dying fire.
  Then winked an eye at the sleeping Squire.
And the shadows around were stealing.

The fox's snout, it moved about,
And loud became the tapping!
  The fox began to howl and bark!
  The fire died down, the room turned dark!
Still louder grew the rapping!

A thundering stroke and the Squire awoke;
He was drowsy, and sore, and sleepy.
  From the shadows above the fox still winked
  At him in his chair as he sat and blinked—
And Anthony Bell felt creepy.

The noise at the door grew more and more!
His knees and his legs were shaky.
  On a sudden the door was opened wide
  To a ghostly figure that stepped inside—
And Anthony Bell grew quaky.

With arms outspread, the ghost then said,
"I come to bring you sorrow;
  For when I appear to one of the Bells,
  As sure as their ancient legend tells,
He then must die on the morrow."

The eyes turned red in the fox's head,
As it wickedly leered in the stillness.
  And Anthony Bell he drew a breath:
  "In what sort of way shall I come by death?
I sure won't die of an illness!"

He began to stamp and rave and ramp,
And the ghost replied "Beware!
  To-morrow you'll come to the Boundary Wall,
  And meet your fate in a fearful fall,
Though you ride your dapple-grey mare."

Up rose the Squire with his eyes afire,
And roared as the ghost was speaking:
  "I'll put my trust in the dapple-grey mare;
  I shan't be killed, and I won't beware,
If I ride till her sides are reeking!"

His anger grew, and he hurled a shoe
Where the ghostly shade was sinking;
  But the ghost was fled, and he flung instead
  His hunting boots at the fox's head.
Roar'd he, "That'll stop thy winking!"

He stood by the door, and cursed and swore
At thought of the ghostly warning.
  Said he: "I fear no Boundary Wall;
  I'll ride the grey, and whate'er befall
She shall carry me up in the morning."

The light was low from the dying glow
Of a candle nearing its socket;
  And he blew his nose in great relief
  With a yellow-and-crimson handkerchief,
Which he pulled from his coat-tail pocket.

With cautious tread he went to bed,
And soundly slept till morning.
  He was up and dressed by seven o'clock,
  As bright as a bean, as firm as a rock,
In spite of his ghostly warning.

The meet that day was not far away;
The sun shone bright and clearly.
  He took his hounds to the covert-side,
  And hummed a tune as he sat astride
The grey which he loved so dearly.

He brushed from her neck a white foam-fleck;
He tightened the girths down under.
  "My dear," said he, "and we'll go to-day;
  And if only our fox runs Moreton way
We'll have that wall, by thunder!"

He threw in his hounds at the lower bounds
Of the Denton long plantation.
  And soon, with a straining, eager dash,
  They were rousing the cover with a crash,
And each rider took up his station.

The fox broke cover down the wind,
And every hound was speaking.
  Then then began such a famous run,
  The finest run that was ever begun;
Each rider his own line seeking.

From the vale below came a loud "Holloa!"
From fat old Farmer Jolly,
  Who viewed the fox as he crossed a lane;
  Then over the brook as he was seen again,
Heading for Steepleton Folly.

They saw the gleam of the Langton Stream,
And went for a bridge up higher.
  The squire sent on the dapple-grey mare,
  And she flew the brook with a yard to spare.
"Begad," said he, "what a flyer!"

From Langton Brook their line they took
From Steepleton on to Rigby;
  And close to his hounds rode Anthony Bell;
  When the tail of the hunt were at Croxton Dell
The Squire was on through Digby.

At Cold Ash Green poor Tom was seen
Down on his head at a double.
  Near Thorndon Hall, though riding light,
  A post and rails stopped Daniel's flight.
And laid him out in a stubble.

Three fields ahead brave Reynard sped;
The hunt was then fast thinning.
  "What a deuce of a run!" said Anthony Bell.
  "When I get home what a tale I'll tell!"
And the fox he looked like winning.

For Moreton Dale, if he didn't fail,
He was saving his strength and cunning.
  Six riders were there who had seen the start,
  The Squire still taking the leading part;
There never was known such running.

He steadied the grey as they led the way;
It was here that he meant to prove her.
  For right ahead was the Boundary Wall,
  All roughly laid, and wide, and tall,
With the tail hounds streaming over.

And he cursed the hosts of all the ghosts
As he rode for his reputation.
  Said he, "I can fall as well as ride."
  And he swore that he'd get to the other side,
If it landed him in damnation.

And straight at the Wall he rode for a fall,
And the grey rolled over her master.
  And pale as a corpse he lay as he fell
  On the sodden wet ground, brave Anthony Bell,
Who had challenged foretold disaster.

. . . . .

When Daniel came he lay the same,
As still as a man that slumbered.
  A farmer brought back the dapple-grey mare,
  And told to Dan with a stony stare
That Squire's days were numbered.

And Dan said: "No, it couldn't be so."
He'd lay him a golden guinea.
  And then, with the help of ploughboys strong,
  The Squire on a gate was borne along
From that spot by Moreton Spinney.

They carried him slow to a farm below;
They sent for Doctor Waters.
  And Daniel returned to Highfield Hall,
  And broke the news of the Squire's fall
To his master's wife and daughters.

They hurried away where the Squire lay,
All of them pale and crying;
  And they found him upstairs in a four-posted bed,
  A little bit dazed and light in the head;
But a very long way from dying.

"He'll never be dead," the Doctor said,
"With six days a week in the saddle;
  If people all lived as hard as he,
  They'd be just as hard as hard could be,
And never a brain would addle."

In a week he was well, was Anthony Bell,
And sitting in Highfield Hall.
  His wife and his daughters were turning pale
  As he got to the end of his wonderful tale
Of the ghost and the Boundary Wall.

"And now," said he, "I wish to see
The chamber they say is haunted."
  And he strode upstairs to the second floor,
  He burst wide open the sealed-up door,
And entered the room undaunted.

He called up Dan, and every man
And all the boys in the stables.
  They turned the closets inside out,
  They searched the house and all about,
From the cellar floor to the gables.

In a cellar bay some burgundy lay
Which the Squire had long forgotten.
  With many a whoop and call they searched
  In the attics above where sparrows perched
On the rafters old and rotten.

High overhead went their noisy tread;
The Squire was down in the spare room,
  When he came on a spring in a panelled door,
  And discovered a chamber unknown before,
Containing a family heirloom.

For a chest stood there in the chamber bare,
Worm-eaten, old, and crazy.
  He broke the locks with blows and knocks,
  He opened the lid of that ancient box;
For a moment his brain was hazy.

Not heeding the noise of the stable-boys,
The Squire was lost in wonder;
  He was handling guineas and bags of gold,
  Necklaces, deeds, and parchments old,
Like a pirate king with his plunder.

For his wife he bawled, his daughters were called;
They should each have a silken gown.
  He'd buy them a chaise, a chaise and pair,
  To drive abroad and take the air!
They should drive to London Town!

And the burgundy came with its ruby flame;
The Squire he roared with pleasure.
  He trod on the tail of his favourite hound;
  He opened a bottle and sent it round,
And they drank success to the treasure.

And it all came true, did that treasure new,
When they sent for Lawyer Berry.
  And after the deeds had all been sought,
  The Parson came in, and they started the port;
There was never a night so merry!

They revelled all night with the diamonds bright;
Each casket swelled the litter!
  They counted the gold until the dawn,
  The necklaces once again were worn,
All in a blazing glitter!

For weeks after that the lawyers sat
In their chambers dim and dusty;
  With searching eye and cautious heed
  They read the lines of each ancient deed
Enrolled in those parchments musty.

And the parchments old produced their gold;
Two footmen stood at the door;
  Each lady was wearing a silken gown;
  They made a long journey to London Town,
And they rode in a chaise and four!

But the Squire of fame remained the same;
He started to hunt on Mondays,
  And he finished up late each Saturday night;
  But his wife and his daughters they claimed the
    right
To take him to church on Sundays.

# FACT AND FICTION

# Florian Performs for Franz Joseph

*from* FLORIAN

*by Felix Salten*

*For 270 years the Lipizzan horses have been trained in the magnificent Spanish Riding School of the Imperial Palace in Vienna.*

*In the time of Franz Joseph, as well as today, the dancing white horses were one of Vienna's major attractions. A gala performance for the emperor or a visiting head of state, as depicted by Felix Salten, was and still is a memorable occasion, not soon to be forgotten by the lucky spectator.*

*During World War II, shortly before the Soviet invasion of Austria, the horses were evacuated to St. Martin in Upper Austria and placed under the protection of General George Patton, U.S. Army, only to be returned to Vienna after the end of the Soviet occupation.*

*Today the Austrian government maintains a stud farm for them, no longer in Lipizza, but in Piber, and in return counts on them to help bring tourists to Vienna.*

*Other books have been written about the Lipizzan horses and Walt Disney made a movie, but this short chapter gives a true feeling of the beauty, pomp, and circumstance of a gala performance in the magnificent Spanish Riding School of the Hofburg.*

*Felix Salten, a native of Vienna, had a distinguished career as a writer of stories and novels about animals. Perhaps his best known work is* Bambi *which, with the aid of a Walt Disney movie, has become a classic.*

*Mr. Salten died in Switzerland in 1946.*

Seven mounted stallions entered and filed in front of the Court Box. Seven bicornes were removed from seven heads, swung to a horizontal position, and replaced.

Florian stood in the center. To his right stood three older stallions, thoroughly trained, and to his left three equally tested ones. He resembled a fiery youth among men. In a row of white steeds he stood out as the only *pure* white one. His snowy skin, unmarred by a single speck, called up memories of cloudless sunny days, of Nature's gracious gifts. His liquid dark eyes, from whose depths his very soul shone forth, sparkled with inner fire and energy and health. Ennsbauer sat in the saddle like a carved image. With his brown frock-coat, his chiseled, reddish brown features and his fixed mien, he seemed to have been poured in metal.

The Emperor had just remarked, "Ennsbauer uses no stirrups or spurs," when the sextet began to play.

The horses walked alongside the grayish-white wainscoting. Their tails were braided with gold, with gold also their waving manes. Pair by pair they were led through the steps of the High School; approached from the far side toward the middle, and went into their syncopated, cadenced stride.

The Emperor had no eyes for any but Florian. Him he watched, deeply engrossed. His connoisseur's eye tested the animal, tested the rider, and could find no flaw that might belie the unstinted praise he had heard showered on them. His right hand played with his mustache, slowly, not with the impatient flick that spelled disappointment over something.

Ennsbauer felt the Emperor's glance like a physical touch. He stiffened. He could hope for no advancement. Nor did he need to fear a fall. Now—in the saddle, under him this unexcelled stallion whose breathing he could feel between his legs and whose readiness and willingness to obey he could sense like some organic outpouring—now doubt and pessimism vanished. The calm, collected, resolute animal gave him calmness, collectedness, resolution.

At last he rode for the applause of the Emperor, of Franz Joseph himself, and by Imperial accolade for enduring fame. Now it was his turn. . . .

Away from the wall he guided Florian, into the center of the ring. An invisible sign, and Florian, as if waiting for it, fell into the Spanish step.

Gracefully and solemnly, he lifted his legs as though one with the rhythm of the music. He gave the impression of carrying his rider collectedly and slowly by his own free will and for his own enjoyment. Jealous of space, he placed one hoof directly in front of the other.

The old Archduke Rainer could not contain himself: "Never have I seen a horse *piaffe* like that!"

Ennsbauer wanted to lead Florian out of the Spanish step, to grant him a moment's respite before the next tour. But Florian insisted on prolonging it, and Ennsbauer submitted.

Florian strode as those horses strode who, centuries ago, triumphantly and conscious of the triumphant occasion, bore Caesars and conquerors into vanquished cities or in homecoming processions. The rigid curved neck, such as ancient sculptors modeled, the heavy short body that seemed to rock on the springs of his legs, the interplay of muscle and joint, together constituted a stately performance, one that amazed the more as it gradually compelled the recognition of its rising out of the will to perfect performance. Every single movement of Florian's revealed nobility, grace, significance and distinction all in one; and in each one of his poses he was an ideal model for a sculptor, the composite of all the equestrian statues of history.

The music continued and Florian, chin pressed against chest, deliberately bowed his head to the left, to the right.

"Do you remember," Elizabeth whispered to her husband, "what our boy once said about Florian? He sings—only one does not hear it."

Ennsbauer also was thinking of the words of little Leopold von Neustift as he led Florian from the Spanish step directly into the *volte.* The delight with which Florian took the change, the effortless ease with which he glided into the short, sharply cadenced gallop, encouraged Ennsbauer to try the most precise and exacting form of the *volte,* the *redoppe,* and to follow that with the *pirouette.*

As though he intended to stamp a circle into the tanbark of the floor, Florian pivoted with his hindlegs fixed to the same place, giving the breath-taking impression of a horse in full gallop that could not bolt loose from the spot, nailed to the ground by a sorcerer or by inner compulsion.

And when, right afterward, with but a short gallop around, Florian rose into the *pesade,* his two forelegs high in the air and hindlegs bent low, and accomplished this difficult feat of balance twice, three times, as if it were child's play, he needed no more spurring on. Ennsbauer simply had to let him be, as he began to *courbette,* stiffly erect. His forelegs did not beat the air, now, but hung limply side by side, folded at the knee. Thus he carried his rider, hopped forward five times without stretching his hindlegs. In the eyes of the spectators Florian's execution of the *courbette* did not impress by its bravura, or by the conquest of body heaviness by careful dressure and rehearsal, but rather as an exuberant means of getting rid of a superabundance of controlled gigantic energy.

Another short canter around the ring was shortened by Florian's own impatience when he involuntarily fell into the

Spanish step. He enjoyed the music, rocked with its rhythm. These men and women and their rank were nothing to him. Still, the presence of onlookers fired him from the very outset. He wanted to please, he had a sharp longing for applause, for admiration; his ambition, goaded on by the music, threw him into a stare of intoxication; youth and fettle raced through his veins like a stream overflowing on a steep grade. Nothing was difficult any longer. With his rider and with all these human beings around him, he celebrated a feast. He did not feel the ground under his feet, the light burden on his back. Gliding, dancing with the melody, he could have flown.

On Florian's back as he hopped on his hindlegs once, twice, Ennsbauer sat stunned, amazed.

Following two successive *croupades,* a tremendous feat, Florian went into the Spanish step still again. Tense and at the same time visibly exuberant, proud and amused, his joyously shining eyes made light of his exertions. From the *ballotade* he thrust himself into the *capriole,* rose high in the air from the standing position, forelegs and hindlegs horizontal. He soared above the ground, his head high in jubilation. Conquering!

Frenetic applause burst out all over the hall, like many fans opening and shutting, like the rustle of stiff paper being torn.

Surrounded by the six other stallions Florian stepped before the Court Box, and while the riders swung their hats in unison, he bowed his proud head just once, conscious, it seemed, of the fact that the ovation was for him and giving thanks in return.

Franz Joseph himself had given the signal for the applause by lightly clapping his hands together. Now he rose and turned to Archduke Rainer, who, as the most distant claimant to the Throne, sat farthest removed from him. Rainer was the oldest among all the archdukes, older even than the seventy-six-year-old Emperor himself. "Well, did you ever see anything like it?" Franz Joseph asked.

# Snow Man: The Farm Horse That Became a Champion

*by Philip B. Kunhardt*

*This is a true, fast-paced story of a horse that was ready for the glue factory and a Long Island riding instructor who teamed up to become the hottest pair on the horse-show open-jumping circuit. This all happened in 1959–1960, but still today, the mention of the name Snow Man brings whistles of appreciation from horse-show aficionados.*

*Philip Kunhardt graduated from Princeton in 1950 and joined* Life *Magazine. Today he is assistant managing editor. He has written on a variety of subjects, from Snow Man to the atomic bomb tests in Nevada, as well as being the author of several children's books.*

If you had been one of the 13,000 spectators at the National Horse Show in New York's Madison Square Garden on November 7, you would have experienced an unexpectedly moving moment. In the middle of the evening the arena was cleared, the lights were dimmed and the band struck up a triumphal march. All eyes followed a spotlight toward the entrance gate at the west end of the ring.

There a big gray horse—obviously not a Thoroughbred—appeared, preceded by five small children. As a blond young man and his wife led the horse to the center of the huge arena, the audience rose and began clapping. In a moment the applause was deafening. The young couple and their children beamed and bowed their thanks, the horse stomped his feet, and the thunderous clapping went on and on.

The horse was Snow Man, and he was being declared the Professional Horsemen's Association champion in open jumping—one of the highest honors the horse-show world has to bestow. That he and his owners, the handsome de Leyer family, were being so wildly cheered was enough to make even the coldest cynic believe in fairy tales.

For, less than four years before, Snow Man had been on his way to the slaughterhouse, a tired farm horse that nobody seemed to want or care about. Fortunately, somebody did care—and this is the story of that caring.

One wintry Monday in February 1956, 28-year-old Harry de Leyer set out from his small riding stable at St. James, Long Island, for the weekly horse auction in New Holland, Pa. Harry had been brought up on a farm in the Netherlands, had always loved horses. In 1950 he married his childhood sweetheart, Joanna Vermeltfoort, and came to the United States. With only a smattering of English, and $160 in capital, Harry and Joanna first tried tobacco farming in North Carolina, then worked on a horse farm in Pennsylvania. Soon the two young Dutch immigrants had a few horses of their own, and within five years Harry was offered the job of riding master at the Knox School for Girls on Long Island. Now the father of three children, he was interested, of course, in doing anything he could to build security for his family.

When Harry headed for the Pennsylvania horse auction that February day, he was aiming to add to his stable for the uses of the school. He arrived late, however; most of the horses had been sold. Wandering outside, he saw several sorry-looking animals being loaded into a butcher's van. These were the "killers"—worn-out work horses that nobody wanted, except the meat dealer. The sight made Harry sad. He felt pity for any horse, however useless, that could not live out his last years in a green pasture.

Suddenly Harry spotted a big gray gelding plodding up the ramp. The horse was chunky, but lighter than the others, and there was a spirited pitch to his ears, a brightness in his eyes. Unaccountably, on instinct alone, de Leyer called to the loader to bring the horse back down.

"You crazy?" said the meat dealer. "He's just an old farm horse."

Probably, Harry thought. The animal's ribs showed, his coat was matted with dirt and manure, there were sores on his legs. Still, there was something about him. . . .

"How much do you want for him?" de Leyer asked.

That's how it all started. Harry de Leyer redeemed an old plug for $80.

The whole de Leyer family was out to greet the horse next day. Down the ramp of the van he came, stumbling over his big feet. He looked slowly about, blinking in the bright winter sun. Then, ankle-deep in snow, covered with shaggy white hair, he stood still as a statue. One of the children said, "He looks just like a snow man." Hence—his name.

They all set about turning Snow Man into a horse again. First they clipped him lightly, and then they washed him—three times. In a while the horseshoer came. Finally, cleaned and curried and shod, Snow Man was ready for his first training session as a riding horse.

Harry laid a dozen thick wooden poles on the ground, spacing them a few feet apart. To walk across the network of poles a horse had to lift his feet high and space his steps. When Snow Man tried it, poles flew every which way, and he stumbled and weaved.

But Snow Man learned fast. By spring he was carrying the novice riders at Knox, and some of the girls even began asking for him in preference to the better-looking horses.

When school closed that summer, Harry de Leyer made what might have been the biggest mistake of his life: he sold Snow Man to a neighborhood doctor for double his money, with the understanding that the doctor would not sell Snow Man, except back to him. After all, Harry told himself, he *was* in the horse business.

Now Snow Man began showing a side that hadn't previously come to light. He insisted on jumping the doctor's fences, no matter how high they were raised, and coming home—cross-country over fields and lawns, through back yards and gardens. Irate citizens called the police. The doctor was glad to let de Leyer have Snow Man back.

The feeling was mutual. For in some strange way de Leyer had come to believe that he and Snow Man shared a common destiny. Solemnly he promised himself never again to part with the horse.

Now, with indication that Snow Man liked to jump, de Leyer began giving him special schooling as a jumper. With kindness and hard work, he helped Snow Man over tougher and tougher obstacles. Finally, in the spring of 1958, he decided to put the big gray to his first real test—at the Sands Point Horse Show on Long Island, where he would compete with some of the top open jumpers in the land.

Incredibly, out on the Sands Point jump course Snow Man seemed able to do no wrong. Again and again spectators held their breath, expecting the ungainly-looking animal to come crashing down on the bars—but he never did. By nightfall of the second day of the three-day show he had achieved the seemingly impossible: he was tied for the lead in the Open Jumper Division with the great old campaigner, Andante.

Then, with success so close, on his final jump of the day Snow Man landed with his feet too close together, and a back hoof slashed his right foreleg. By tomorrow it would be swollen and stiff. But de Leyer isn't one to give up easily. He cut a section out of a tire tube, slipped it over Snow Man's injured leg like a sock, tied up the bottom and filled the top with ice. All night long he kept the improvised sock full of fresh ice, told Snow Man over and over how they would win next day.

When morning came, the leg was neither stiff nor swollen. And on the final round of the day Snow Man beat the mighty Andante!

Harry de Leyer now saw that he had a potential champion—possibly even a national champion. But giving Snow Man a chance to prove it meant hitting the horse-show circuit in earnest, vanning to a new show each week-end, putting up big entry fees, riding his heart out—a long, tiring summer and autumn that *could* end in little reward. Moreover, a spot on Harry's tongue had begun to hurt, and to worry him. It would be easier to forget about championships. Still, after talking it over, Harry and Joanna decided that Snow Man deserved a try.

So, to Connecticut they went. Snow Man won at the Fairfield Horse Show and at Lakeville. Then to Branchville, N. J.—but Harry was in no condition to ride a winner. His tongue had begun to bother him badly, and he had scarcely eaten for a week; Snow Man had a bad day. Blaming himself for the big jumper's first loss, Harry de Leyer drove home that Sunday night gritting his teeth against his pain.

On Monday he went to a doctor. On Tuesday he entered a Long Island hospital to have a tumor removed from his tongue. On Saturday he got the laboratory report: the tumor was malignant. It was the end of the life he had known, the end of Snow Man's quest for glory.

Harry drove to the Smithtown Horse Show, a few miles from his home, making plans to sell his horses. But somehow he would keep Snow Man. The horse would be turned out to pasture.

Sitting at the show, de Leyer heard his name annouced over the loud-speaker: he was to go home immediately. Harry's first thought was: the children! His second: a fire! He sped home, wondering how much more a man could take. But when he turned into the driveway, the children were playing in the yard and there stood the house. Joanna was close to hysteria, however. A message had come from the hospital that Harry's laboratory report had been mixed up with another; the tumor was not malignant!

"All of a sudden," Harry says, "my life was handed back to me."

From then on the summer and early fall became one happy rush toward more and more championships at important shows. And finally it was November, time for the biggest show of all—the National at Madison Square Garden.

The National Horse Show lasts eight days. Horses that lack either consistency or stamina are weeded out long before the final night. After seven days Snow Man was tied in the Open Jumper Division with a chestnut mare, First Chance. For their jump-off on the eighth day the course was long and intricate. It weaved around the Garden oval in four overlapping loops; it included quick turns and changes of direction—combinations which call for perfect timing and coordination.

First Chance went first. Whether it was the tenseness of the moment, the wear and tear from so many days of jumping, or the difficulties of the course, no one can be sure. At any rate, First Chance "knocked" several barriers.

Now it was up to Snow Man to run a cleaner course. Slowly he headed for the first jump. De Leyer nudged him with his knees, and the big gray exploded over it. Now up and over Snow Man went, and up and over again. Over the brush jump, over the chicken coop, the hog's-back, the bull's-eye, the striped panel. There were a few touches, but far fewer than First Chance had made. Finally he approached the last jump.

Now Harry de Leyer sat up in the saddle and threw the reins across the horse's neck. He was showing, for everyone to see, that it was not he who was responsible for this great performance, that it was the horse. Snow Man rumbled up to that final jump, and he thrust and he sailed and it was done! An old and unpedigreed farm horse had won it all—the National Horse Show Open Jumper Championship, the Professional Horsemen's Association Trophy and the American Horse Shows Association High Score Award. He was declared "Horse of the Year" in open jumping.

Then, last year, Snow Man was "Horse of the Year" once more. And if you had been one of the vast crowd that filled Madison Square Garden that November evening to watch the de Leyer family and their big gray receive the ovation, you, too, would have stood . . . and clapped . . . and perhaps even cried—for the victory of a horse and a man who cared.

# The Will

*from* A KINGDOM IN A HORSE

*by Maia Wojciechowska*

*Excerpts are always difficult, but this short chapter will give you an opportunity to enjoy a few pages of perhaps the most beautifully written current American horse story.*

*Superbly executed by Maia Wojciechowska, the 1965 winner of the Newberry Medal for children's literature,* A Kingdom in a Horse *tells of the love of a boy, a horse, and a lonely old woman.*

*Born in Warsaw, the author attended schools in Poland, France, and England before coming to this country in 1942. Several years ago Miss Wojciechowska and her daughter Oriana, moved into New York City from New Jersey, where they owned a horse very much like Gypsy, the equine heroine of* A Kingdom in a Horse.

What if—" David asked his father as they approached the woman's house, "what if Doc Smith says it's founder?"

"If it is," his father replied slowly, "I don't think Mrs. Tierney will be able to bear to see Gypsy suffer. The first time she hears Gypsy groan, and sees her sweat and refuse to get up—"

"She hasn't foundered!" David shouted then, not wanting his father to go on.

They were waiting, Gypsy wearing her blanket and the woman a warm coat in which she seemed to shiver.

"Can I ride in the trailer?" she wanted to know.

"It's too small," Lee said.

Into the built-in feeder Sarah put some hay and grains and a few handfuls of lettuce leaves. They had no trouble getting Gypsy into the trailer, but her legs seemed very weak and her walk stiff-kneed. They didn't talk much on the way to Burlington, but just before turning into Dr. Smith's driveway Sarah said, "I've read about laminitis in the *Horseman's Encyclopedia*. It didn't say that it's incurable, but it did say about the pain. Do they recover?"

"Sometimes," Lee said.

"I think," Sarah said quietly, "that it might be better if she didn't have to suffer."

Dr. Smith, a giant of a man, watched as Gypsy backed out of the trailer and walked toward the stable.

"She walks so much better!" Sarah whispered in awe. And indeed Gypsy's walk, although not perfect, was remarkably improved.

"That often happens," Dr. Smith said, his eyes on the horse as it was being led around by Lee. "When they brace themselves in the trailer they're using muscles that they didn't even know they had."

"Then it's not founder!" Sarah exclaimed.

"Why does every horse owner," Dr. Smith asked no one in particular, "always think the animal's foundered? To me this looks as if she's pulled a tendon on her right foot and has been favoring the other. Did you bring the bridle with you?"

"No," David said, "but if you want me to trot her on the pavement, I could do it without one."

"You know a lot about horses, don't you?" Dr. Smith said,

smiling as David hoisted himself on Gypsy's back. "That's the very best way to check on a pulled tendon, by trotting the animal on hard pavement."

Gypsy didn't have to trot far for the doctor to confirm his diagnosis.

"You'll be all right!" Sarah was saying loudly, hugging Gypsy, burying her face in the horse's neck.

"It could have happened anytime, couldn't it?" David was asking the doctor.

"Sure. She could even have pulled it getting up in the stall or walking in the pasture. It can happen sometimes when they shift weight while they're standing still. Of course," he looked at David and smiled, "if you've been riding her over very rough terrain, it could be your fault."

"But she'll be all right, won't she?" Sarah was asking.

"She'll be all right," the doctor answered, "only if you take good care of her. I'll give her a shot of cortisone. Lee will pull off her shoes, and she'll need plenty of rest, some walking on a lead line and daily soaking of her right foot in Epsom salts. Later on she might need special heeled shoes, but maybe she'll recover so completely that that won't be necessary. She shouldn't be ridden, of course, and by Christmas she should be as good as new." He pried open Gypsy's mouth. "She's sixteen, and by spring she could be in good enough shape to be in foal again."

The cure began that very same day. Lee devised a plastic stocking which kept the hot compresses warm. David managed to find a battery-powered massager which helped the circulation of the blood in Gypsy's legs. Now each day after school David would bicycle over to Sarah's house. Together they would attend to Gypsy. They would baby her as if the very fact that she had not foundered was something that they had to reward with constant care and abounding love. Their common attention to the horse drew them close together, and neither one could any longer imagine life without the other.

"Just a short while ago," David told Sarah one day, "I didn't care about the future or anything much. But now I know what it is that I want to do with my life. I'll study to be a vet. But that's not the important part. Do you want to guess what the most important thing in my life is going to be?"

"It has something to do with horses, doesn't it?"

"Yes, but you'd never guess!" His eyes were bright on her. "I want to have a sort of nursing home for old horses. You know, a place where the very old ones, the ones that can no longer be ridden, or work, or anything, can come to rest. I want to give them a good time before they die. I will go to auctions and find those that should no longer be used, and I'll buy them and bring them to this place I'll have, a farmlike place, with great big pastures, lots of shade and water. They will have the best of care, because I'll be a vet then, and lots of company and good food, and no one will be riding them or working them. They will just lead lazy lives and be so spoiled that if they were ever abused they will no longer remember. And I'll even advertise, in all sorts of newspapers and magazines, that I'll take old horses and keep them for nothing so that even people who are good to their animals but don't know what to do with them when they grow old can send me theirs. And it won't be a sad place. It will be big and the horses will feel free, and they will graze over acres of green grass and there will be no one asking them to do anything."

Even before he stopped talking she knew he need not wait to grow up. She could make his dream a reality.

"Oh, David!" she shouted, hugging him. "This farm, wouldn't it make a perfect place? The barn is there. It used to house forty cows once. If we make box stalls, we could have twenty horses there, at least, and there are streams running through the fields and plenty of trees for shade. All we'd need do would be to fence the whole thing in. Isn't it perfect?"

They were laughing and making their plans when Lee drove

in to pick up David. When they told him what they were planning to do he was immediately carried away by the idea.

"It wouldn't take hardly any work at all," he said. "We could hire a few of the boys from your school to help us with the fencing—"

"There're the twins, and Peter Pollock," David interrupted. "I know they'd help us—"

"And the barn," Lee went on, "it's in great shape except it would need a wooden floor and partitions, but I know of a place where I can pick up the lumber, used planks, for next to nothing, and there is also an old house that they wanted to burn down, and I can get the flooring off that."

"We'll start in the spring," Sarah said and laughed. "By the summer, by the beginning of summer we will have our first horse, and Gypsy will have company."

"She won't ever be jealous," David assured her, "because her stable will always be her very own, and the others will realize she's a queen here."

That evening when David and his father had gone back to their own house, Sarah sat down to write her will. She left her property and all her money, her husband's insurance and her own, as well as her small income, to Lee in trust for David, to be used for what she called "a horse kingdom." And that night she dreamt again, and remembered the dream when she woke up. She had dreamt of horses, old, misused horses, acres of them, feeding on grass, sunbathing, nuzzling each other, moving slowly, some running, others standing still, as if lost in dreams; and among them stood Gypsy with a foal by her side.

# It's My Own Invention

*from* THROUGH THE LOOKING GLASS

*by Lewis Carroll*

*These few lines from Lewis Carroll's immortal* Through The Looking Glass *well exemplify his combination of the fantastic with familiar details of everyday life. Perhaps scanning these pages will give you the incentive to reread* Carroll's Alice in Wonderland *and* Through the Looking Glass, *which most of us read too young and have never fully appreciated.*

*Lewis Carroll was the pseudonym of Charles Ludwidge Dodgson, 1832–1898, a lecturer in higher mathematics at Christ College, Oxford.*

*Dodgson, or Carroll, liked children and developed the Alice stories from the tales he told a colleague's youngsters. As Alice, daughter of Dean Liddell, was his favorite, she became the heroine of his books.*

*Today Dodgson's mathematical work,* Euclid and His Modern Rivals *(1879), has been forgotten, but Alice's Adventures are as popular, if not more popular, with children of all ages, than they were when they were first published in the eighteen-sixties.*

Whenever the horse stopped (which it did very often), he fell off in front; and, whenever it went on again (which it generally did rather suddenly), he fell off behind. Otherwise he kept on pretty well, except that he had a habit of now and then falling off sideways; and as he generally did this on the side on which Alice was walking, she soon found that it was the best plan not to walk *quite* close to the horse.

"I'm afraid you've not had much practice in riding," she ventured to say, as she was helping him up from his fifth tumble.

The Knight looked very much surprised, and a little offended at the remark. "What makes you say that?" he asked, as he scrambled back into the saddle, keeping hold of Alice's hair with one hand, to save himself from falling over on the other side.

"Because people don't fall off quite so often, when they've had much practice."

"I've had plenty of practice," the Knight said very gravely: "plenty of practice!"

Alice could think of nothing better to say than "Indeed?" but she said it as heartily as she could. They went on a little way in silence after this, the Knight with his eyes shut, muttering to himself, and Alice watching anxiously for the next tumble.

"The great art of riding," the Knight suddenly began in a loud voice, waving his right arm as he spoke, "is to keep——" Here the sentence ended as suddenly as it had begun, as the Knight fell heavily on the top of his head exactly in the path where Alice was walking. She was quite frightened this time, and said in an anxious tone, as she picked him up, "I hope no bones are broken?"

"None to speak of," the Knight said, as if he didn't mind breaking two or three of them. "The great art of riding, as I was saying, is—to keep your balance properly. Like this, you know——"

He let go the bridle, and stretched out both his arms to show

Alice what he meant, and this time he fell flat on his back, right under the horse's feet.

"Plenty of practice!" he went on repeating, all the time that Alice was getting him on his feet again. "Plenty of practice!"

"It's too ridiculous!" cried Alice, losing all her patience this time. "You ought to have a wooden horse on wheels, that you ought!"

"Does that kind go smoothly?" the Knight asked in a tone of great interest, clasping his arms round the horse's neck as he spoke, just in time to save himself from tumbling off again.

"Much more smoothly than a live horse," Alice said, with a little scream of laughter, in spite of all she could do to prevent it.

"I'll get one," the Knight said thoughtfully to himself. "One or two—several."